*Zach never had—
enter a relations...*

Too many pitfalls, too many complications, too big of a chance that management would think he had his mind on something other than the job.

Unfortunately, Zach hadn't forgotten the first time he met Allison. That first smile, that first touch…

She's never let me forget, he thought. Just the sound of her laughter drifting down the hall made his gut clench and sent an electric rush of energy charging through his veins.

And every time she smiled at him, the flash of that dimple reminded him of his weakness where she was concerned, reminded him she was a woman who could do what no other woman had ever done—take his mind off his career.

Dear Reader,

Once upon a time, I took a job at a temp agency. I failed miserably, in that my first "temporary" assignment turned into a long-term, permanent position. I had no idea that would be the case, but I was lucky everything turned out as it did.

Allison Warner took a far bigger chance when she followed her boyfriend to New York for a new job, but it was a move she soon regretted. Now, she's determined to keep things simple—working at a temp agency, where she won't make the mistake of mixing her personal and professional life again.

But life and love are rarely simple, and Allison's life gets a lot more complicated when she agrees to a one-night-only pretend date with her secret crush, Zach Wilder. Little does Allison realize where that one night will take them….

I hope you enjoy Allison and Zach's story as they work together to find a lasting love!

Stacy Connelly

TEMPORARY BOSS...
FOREVER HUSBAND

STACY CONNELLY

Harlequin

SPECIAL EDITION

Recycling programs
for this product may
not exist in your area.

ISBN-13: 978-0-373-65630-1

TEMPORARY BOSS...FOREVER HUSBAND

Printed in U.S.A.

Books by Stacy Connelly

Harlequin Special Edition

Her Fill-In Fiancé #2128
Temporary Boss...Forever Husband #2148

Silhouette Special Edition

All She Wants for Christmas #1944
Once Upon a Wedding #1992
The Wedding She Always Wanted #2033

STACY CONNELLY

has dreamed of publishing books since she was a kid, writing stories about a girl and her horse. Eventually, boys made it onto the page as she discovered a love of romance and the promise of happily ever after.

When she is not lost in the land of make-believe, Stacy lives in Arizona with her two spoiled dogs. She loves to hear from readers and can be contacted at stacyconnelly@cox.net or www.stacyconnelly.com.

I can't remember the very first romance I ever picked up
or attempt a guess at how many I have read since,
but this is dedicated to all the authors
whose books I have enjoyed over the years.

Thank you.

Chapter One

Allison Warner counted the rings as she waited for her sister to pick up the phone. After the fourth, she heard the all too familiar click of her call going through to voice mail—again. Bethany's voice came across the line, advising Allison to leave a message.

Allison sighed, giving in to the disappointment that had shadowed her since she'd moved back to Arizona five months ago. She'd talked to Bethany's voice mail more than she'd talked to her sister, and she didn't know which frustrated her more—the message Bethany would likely ignore or the caller ID that enabled Bethany to ignore her call in the first place. Still, she took a deep breath and forced a bright note into her voice.

"Hi, Bethany. It's Allison—your sister," she teased even though the words really weren't funny. "It's Thursday afternoon, and I'm getting ready to leave work. I was calling to see if you wanted to go out for dinner tonight or maybe shopping this weekend. We could look for baby furniture or decorations for the nursery. I'm free all weekend if you feel up to hitting the mall. Or we could look online if you're not up to going out. So, you know, just call me."

Allison cringed as she hung up the phone. Could she have sounded any more desperate? And hadn't she learned by now, the harder she tried, the more Bethany resisted?

You have to be patient. The break in their relationship hadn't happened overnight. Allison would be foolish to hope she could repair the damage in a snap. *It's going to take time.*

Fortunately, that was one thing Allison had plenty of on her hands. After shutting down her computer, she took a moment to straighten the few personal items on her desk. The misshapen coffee mug she'd thrown in pottery class; the wilting African violet; the handcrafted picture frame that rained tiny glass beads any time she picked it up. She and her sister smiled out from the photograph, heads tilted together in perfect symmetry. A single, perfect moment caught in time...

If only life had that kind of pause button, to freeze a moment she wanted to last...or better yet, a rewind button, so she could go back in time, and undo her poor choices.

The picture had been taken at Bethany's wedding when the two sisters were as close as could be. Bittersweet memories of the ceremony and the last time her family had been together flashed through Allison's mind. Bethany had smiled with tears in her eyes as their father walked her down the aisle and handed her to Gage Armstrong. Allison had stood at her sister's side, her maid of honor and best friend.

Only a few weeks later, Allison had followed her boyfriend, Kevin Hodges, to New York. That had been three years ago, and three years was a long time. Long enough for their father's health to fail, for Bethany's marriage to fall apart and for Allison to get so wrapped up in her career that she'd been oblivious to both. She had moved back home, but the three thousand mile gap had been much easier to close than the emotional distance between Allison and her sister. Especially when Bethany had made her opinion so clear.

Too little, too late.

Guilt pressed against Allison's chest, the truth in her sister's words weighing so heavily it hurt to breathe. She'd give anything, *anything* to turn back the clock and to be with her family when they'd needed her most. But that time was gone, and the only thing that kept Allison going was her determination to make the most of *now*.

"You have to get Bethany to open up and talk about what went wrong with her and Gage," their mother had insisted before she left on her three-week Mexican cruise. The trip was one Allison's parents had long planned to make for their thirty-fifth anniversary. When her father passed away six months before the anniversary date, Allison's mother decided to take the trip anyway as a tribute to his memory.

She missed her father so much. His laughter, his love, his encouragement to always aim high and shoot for the stars. How he would hate that his death had driven a wedge between his daughters. His girls, as he'd fondly referred to Bethany, Allison, and their mother. It would have broken his heart. And though Bethany refused to believe it, the loss of their once-close relationship broke Allison's heart, too.

Setting the picture frame back on her desk, she sighed. She couldn't change the past, but she was determined to do whatever it took to rebuild her relationship with her sister. Right now, Bethany needed family around her more than ever, whether she'd admit it or not.

At five-thirty, the offices of Knox Security were mostly empty, and she took a moment to walk down the hall and turn off the lights. She could have left a half an hour ago, but she'd wanted to finish up some filing for what would be the last full week of her temporary assignment at the security-systems firm.

On Monday, Martha Scanlon would be back after a two-month absence for hip replacement surgery. Allison would return for a day or two to catch the woman up on everything that had been started during her sick leave. After that, she would move on to another temporary assignment.

The receptionist job at Knox Security had been her longest to date. Normally, she filled in for only a week or two, subbing for vacationing employees or emergency situations. She liked the variety of working as a temp, liked the short-term nature of the jobs. The Monday through Friday, eight-to-five schedule was a world away from the sixty-hour-a-week grind she'd gotten used to working for Marton/Mills, an advertising firm in New York City. There was no chance of getting caught up in climbing the corporate ladder, on focusing so much on professional goals that personal relationships were pushed aside.

The glow of a glorious sunset shone outside the office window, signaling the end of another gorgeous spring day. One more reason to enjoy working in her hometown. The April weather was beautiful, sunny and warm and perfect for shorts and T-shirts. Business casual wasn't *that* casual even in Phoenix, and though Allison had left her razor-cut suits behind in New York, she did her best to dress appropriately while still being herself.

If you want to get ahead, you're going to have to learn to dress the part.

The echo of her ex-boyfriend's words still burned as did the memory of how she'd so eagerly buried every bit of her own personality to force herself into a corporate mold. She'd tried so hard to be the perfect girlfriend, the perfect rising star employee. Kevin had been the chosen one, the young graduate whose father was good friends with the CEO at Barton/Mills. She'd tagged along as little more than a "plus one" on Kevin's job offer, determined to be so much more. Starting at the bottom, she'd expected to pay the professional price of hard work and long hours, but she never imagined the personal costs.

Never again would she lose herself in a job or in a man, and her choice of wardrobe was a daily reminder.

Today, she'd worn a pin-striped black skirt and black knit mock turtleneck—a perfectly respectable combination, but one kept from being *too* boring by the barely-there pink lace at the hem of the skirt. It was a recent purchase, and one she'd been eager to wear that day. Not that she had any particular reason to choose an outfit that did the most to compliment her short blond hair and green eyes. No reason at all…

Her steps gradually slowed and her pulse quickened as she neared Zach Wilder's office. After two months, she should have been used to the sight of his dark hair, vibrant blue eyes and chiseled features. Even his broad shoulders, narrow waist and lean, muscular limbs should have been commonplace by now. Still, there was something about the company's lead salesman that stole her breath every single time their paths crossed. That Zach was as wrong for her as a man could be did *nothing* to cool the attraction.

The old saying was true—you never have a second chance to make a first impression, and Allison's first impression of Zach had been one of…possibility. They'd met briefly her first day at Knox with an incidental touch in the elevator that had rocked her to the soles of her stylish pumps. Weeks later, she felt like she was still reeling. As if that momentary encounter had done more than set her back on her heels, as if it had somehow thrown her off her emotional axis, threatening to send her life spinning in a different direction.

It was crazy to put so much importance on a mundane event, but Allison knew she hadn't imagined the moment. Nor had she imagined the spark of attraction or the answering awareness burning in Zach Wilder's blue eyes. Their first meeting still teased her thoughts with only the slightest provocation. Just the sound of his deep voice sent the memory shivering down her spine. But it was everything that happened *after* that meeting Allison forced herself to remember.

As in his reputation of business first—period. As in Zach keeping such a tight and narrow focus on work that she never again crossed into his line of sight.

Too bad Allison hadn't had as easy a time ignoring Zach. Each time she walked by his office, she couldn't resist sneaking a peek inside. She'd made a study of the way his blue eyes narrowed when he stared at the computer screen. The way his jaw clenched when something went wrong and the way the corner of his mouth kicked into a half smile when things went right.

But what she noticed most were the rare moments when sheer exhaustion hit. When Zach would rub eyes aching from the strain of staring at the computer and roll his head back on his shoulders, no doubt trying to dislodge the burden of constantly trying to succeed.

In those brief periods of time, Allison felt she was seeing the real Zach Wilder. He seemed...human. Vulnerable.

Fortunately, that didn't happen often or last more than a split second before Zach immediately snapped back into business mode, seeming determined to wipe out any hint of weakness.

But like the bad habit it was, Allison glanced inside the narrow glass window alongside the door. His chair was pushed back from his desk as if awaiting his return, but the room was empty. She was a little surprised. From the moment she started at Knox, she'd heard all about the long hours he worked, the impossible accounts he won, the fast track he was taking at breakneck speed. Each word shot off a warning flare in Allison, illuminating the danger of a man who was driven, ambitious and willing to succeed at all costs. But along with every accomplishment, Allison heard the undeniable respect and admiration of his fellow employees for a man who'd worked his way up through the ranks to earn the position he held.

That alone was a world away from the friend-of-the-family connections Kevin had used for a significant leg up on the ladder of success.

But despite their differences, Zach still shared enough similarities with her ex-boyfriend to send Allison running... even if he was so gorgeous she couldn't resist taking a look back.

Good thing she only had a few days left at Knox. She'd move on to the next job and leave all thoughts of Zach behind. She ran a finger across the brass placard, tracing his name, until she realized what she was doing and snatched her hand back. She hurried down the hall, embarrassed and relieved no one had had seen her mooning over Zach Wilder's door.

Tuesday could not come soon enough, she thought as she stepped inside the waiting elevator and hit the button for the garage.

The doors had nearly closed when a masculine hand reached inside. One glance at the long, lean fingers, starched white cuff and designer watch, and a small shiver rippled from head to toe. She recognized that watch. She'd picked it out herself, on instructions from her boss, as a gift to the salesman of the year five years running.

Allison braced for what she already knew was coming, but try as she might, she couldn't keep her breath from catching when the silvered doors opened like an unveiling of female fantasies come to life and Zach Wilder stepped inside the elevator.

Five o'clock shadow darkened his jaw, matching the hint of circles beneath his eyes. A lock of dark hair fell across his forehead, and his red and black geometric tie was off-kilter.

"Zach, is everything all right?" She'd never seen him look so disheveled. He looked—he looked like she pictured he would after being kissed. Because what woman could resist running her hands through his dark hair? Or using his always perfectly knotted tie to pull him closer? And wouldn't she love to put that hint of desperation in his blue eyes?

Allison's face heated at the foolish direction of her own thoughts. Like Zach would ever make out with someone at work! She knew better than that. Just like she knew better than to even entertain such a fantasy when he was standing so close. She twisted her fingers together as if she might grab hold of the thoughts running loose inside her mind. The last thing she needed was for all-business Zach to guess she had such an unprofessional crush on him.

His blue eyes drilled into hers as the elevator doors slid closed behind him. Slightly out of breath from running to catch the elevator, he confessed, "I was afraid I was going to miss you."

"Miss me?" She was afraid she would miss him too, but even as distracted as she was by being so close to him, Allison didn't think he meant the words the same way she did.

She wanted to take a step back, to give herself some breathing room free of the enticing scent of his citrus and spice cologne. But the elevator was too small and his presence too overwhelming for Allison to escape. And maybe it was time to confront her ridiculous crush—and Zach—head on. "You didn't miss me. I'm right here. Is there something you need?"

"I need you."

Her heart slammed into her chest at the confession. Her stomach dropped to her high heels before bouncing back up again, and she didn't think it had anything to do with the elevator's gradual descent. "I—you what?"

"I need your help with a client."

"Oh, right. A client."

Embarrassment flooded through her. What exactly had she thought Zach was confessing? Some deep, emotional need? Please! The man lived and breathed work. She *knew* that. So why had she so quickly jumped to such a ridiculous conclusion? And why would she even consider testing the waters of her attraction for him when she knew how it would end? Business would win hands down and she'd be so far behind, she wouldn't even show up in the picture.

"Can this wait until tomorrow? I'm kind of off the clock."

He was shaking his head before she finished speaking. "No, it's an emergency," he declared as the elevator doors opened to the parking garage. He caught her hand and started pulling her down the aisle of cars, leaving her little choice but to trot alongside. "I need you to come with me."

Late in the day and with the security lights not yet on, the parking garage was cloaked in shadows. Keeping pace beside Zach, Allison felt like she'd stepped into a spy thriller. Any moment, bad guys would jump out and spray the surrounding cars with a volley of bullets. Despite the slightly dangerous air and her own overactive imagination, they reached his car unscathed.

Almost unscathed, Allison amended, feeling the imprint of his palm branding hers. That slow burn inched up her arm, across her torso, tightening her breasts and centering in her heart.

"Emergency? People have medical emergencies, mechanical emergencies, plumbing emergencies. They don't have receptionist emergencies! There's no such thing—"

"I'll pay you overtime. Double time...triple time. Whatever you want."

"It's after five-thirty. I want to go home." Of course, going home meant hanging out alone because, despite the message she left, her sister wouldn't call back. But she was *not* a workaholic. Not anymore. She refused to sacrifice everything for money or success or whatever demons drove Zach.

He halted beside a black BMW and turned to face her. "Please."

That single word, one she sensed Zach didn't say often, swayed her. A razor-sharp determination always ran beneath his polished surface, but today that edge was slicing through the façade, revealing the real man inside. *That* was the man who caught her attention. The real man she sensed was buried so deep few people ever saw a hint of him. And this might be Allison's last and only chance to see more...

Ignoring the warning in her head, she conceded, "Okay, I'll help. What do you need?"

"I'll explain on the way."

"On the way where?"

"Where we're going," he said cryptically as he opened the passenger door.

She should be at least a little annoyed by his arrogance. After all, she was the one helping him, not the other way around. But a quick check of the emotions ping-ponging through her body as she slid into the leather seat, and nope, not an annoyed ball in the mix. Just curiosity and attraction bouncing back and forth, jumping through her stomach and along her nerve endings.

Zach didn't speak as he drove, the traffic-filled streets slowly taking them toward Scottsdale. Now that she'd agreed to help, he seemed willing to keep her completely in the dark when it came to *how* she was supposed to do that. Fidgeting with the beads on her purse, she kept quiet as long as she could before bursting out. "If I'm going to help you, you'll have to tell me what you need."

Stopped at a red light, he glanced over at her. Their eyes met, and questions about what Zach *needed* to break through the stress and tension constantly pulling at him tempted

Allison. She knew it had to be a trick of the setting sun that a spark of desire in his blue eyes seemed to answer those questions...

The honk of a horn behind them jerked Zach's attention forward once more, freeing her from the intensity of his gaze. Allison exhaled a sigh of relief as she practically wilted against the seat. She didn't know what the rest of the night had in store, but she'd never survive it if she kept letting her imagination run away with her.

"I have a dinner meeting in half an hour," he said, his grim tone a sharp contrast to the simple statement.

"Okay," she said slowly. "That watch of yours tells me you're usually a little more excited about meeting with clients."

Everything she knew about Zach Wilder told Allison he was a man who lived for the hunt, that victory—and conquest—could never live up to the chase. All the more reason to stay out of his sights, but she sensed his desperation, a chink in Zach's normally impenetrable armor. And not that she was searching for a weakness, but somehow, she couldn't let this opportunity go.

"You've had tough clients before. What about this dinner has you so stressed?"

Zach winced. "I'm not supposed to be so easy to read."

"Oh, don't worry. You're a total mystery," she said wryly. On one hand, Zach was an open book. Or, more like an open business journal—focused on one thing and one thing only. As for the reasons why...Allison was completely in the dark. "But why aren't you more excited?"

"I am excited," Zach protested, his shoulders straightening against the padded leather seat in a defensive stance. "This was supposed to be my second meeting with James and Riana Collins of Collins Jewelers. James recently moved to Scottsdale, planning to hand over the reins of his company, but his retirement only lasted a few months. Now, instead of taking a step back, he's decided to expand his stores to the Southwest, starting in Scottsdale and Las Vegas, and I've got a good shot at winning the security contract for Knox."

"Sounds great. What's the catch?"

His hands tightened on the wheel as if he thought the car might be the next thing to spin out of his control. "Riana left a message that James can't make it."

"But you can still meet with her."

With a dark and emphatic scowl, he muttered, "Exactly."

A burst of understanding hit her. "So it's like that, is it?" Allison couldn't blame any woman for finding Zach attractive, but she had little respect for anyone who would cheat on a spouse. Her parents' marriage had shown her what a union built on love and trust could be like, and she clung to that ideal even if her own relationship with Kevin had fallen woefully short. He might not have cheated on her, but he was still a cheat.

Shoving thoughts of her ex aside, Allison said to Zach, "I'm sure Mrs. Collins—"

"Ms. Collins," Zach interrupted. "Riana is James's daughter."

"Oh," Allison said, as her mental image of James Collins as an outraged husband altered to overprotective father, and Riana from cougar to kitten. "Still, Ms. Collins can't be the first admirer you've had. You must know how to let a girl down easy."

Even as she said the words, she wondered if they were true. Was Zach the type to send flowers along with an "it's not you, it's me" note? Or was he more the kind of guy who simply stopped calling?

Not that it mattered; she wasn't considering a relationship with Zach. At least, not *seriously* considering one.

"That's different. Riana Collins isn't someone I met in a

bar. This is business." He underscored the word with such emphasis, words like HUGE, IMPORTANT or EVERYTHING could have been used in its place. "Turning her down could offend her. If I so much as hurt her feelings, it could end this deal. And I will not let that happen."

"Well…" Allison pretended to think for a minute. "I suppose you could always sleep with her."

"That's something else I won't let happen," he said.

Because sleeping with the client's daughter could do more professional harm in the long run? Or because using a woman went against his morals? She wanted to believe his resistance to Riana Collins showed his true character, that as important as business was to him, he had boundaries. That he was determined to succeed, but not at all costs. That was what Allison wanted to believe, but truthfully, she didn't know.

The wanting should have worried her as well as the reason behind it. She would never make the mistake of falling for a man like Kevin Hodges again, but if she was wrong about Zach, if he proved himself different from her avaricious, scheming ex, would that be a green light to the attraction she felt? An okay to ignore the warning signs telling her to stay far, far away and to listen to the pulse of desire that urged her closer anytime Zach came near?

If he was different…maybe tonight would be her chance to safely find out. After all, Zach had already set the ground rules.

"Okay, so no mixing business with pleasure," Allison stated.

It would be a reminder to herself as well as the on-the-prowl Ms. Collins. Because sitting in Zach's car, the scent of the leather seats and his aftershave riding on the warm breeze blowing through his open window, Allison could too easily imagine this was a date. That Zach was taking her to some romantic, elegant restaurant. A seductive shiver ran through her as she imagined him focusing that driven, intense gaze on wooing and winning *her* instead of yet another business deal…

"No."

Zach's abrupt denial slapped the daydream right out of her head. "What?" she asked defensively.

He slanted her a questioning look. "I was agreeing with you. No mixing business with pleasure."

"Right. Of course not. Strictly professional." As professional as she could be with her mental pants on fire. "So I'm here to…what? Chaperone?"

"Something like that," he muttered, giving Allison the idea that he might have another plan in mind.

Still, she had agreed, and it was only one night… "You know the old saying, two's company, three's a crowd?"

"Yeah," he said, slowly dragging out the word.

Allison smiled. "I'm your crowd."

Chapter Two

Zach had known Allison Warner was trouble the first time he saw her. Problem was, the first time he saw her, he had no idea she was the temp hired to fill in for the company's hospitalized receptionist.

How could he have known? She certainly hadn't looked *anything* like a replacement for matronly Martha Scanlon. He supposed Allison had dressed professionally enough— she'd been wearing a cotton candy-soft, pale blue sweater and matching geometric print skirt—but she'd immediately caught his eye as she cut in front of his car in the parking garage with a wink and a wave. Even in the dim light of the underground garage, her short hair boasted every shade of blond under the sun. From dark to caramel to platinum, the strands blended together in tousled perfection, a gorgeous compliment to her golden skin and elegant features.

It would have been easy to label her cute or sweet, but something in that wink told Zach this was one angel with a devil on her shoulder.

He'd spun into the closest parking space, mentally insisting he was hurrying back to the office, yet knowing it was a lie. He caught up with her at the elevator. Glancing over her shoulder, her smile seemed to say she'd been waiting for him. "Going up?" she teased, hitting the only button available.

His thoughts took a turn in the opposite direction as he caught sight of the dimple in her right cheek when she smiled. That single dimple, rather than the typical matched pair, seemed to hint at the woman's unique take on life, and Zach sensed she was someone who could always find the humor in a situation even if it meant laughing at herself.

He opened his mouth, ready to respond with a clever, sophisticated remark, only to catch another glimpse of her smile and find himself completely tongue-tied. "I, um, yeah."

Of course you're going up. You're in an underground parking garage, idiot!

The woman's eyes sparkled, telling Zach she certainly had no problem laughing at *him*.

Accompanied by the ping of the bell, the elevator doors swung open, and Zach gestured for her to precede him, determined to use the short ride as an opportunity to recover his masculine pride. His mother Caroline was always telling him he needed to get a life. To her, that meant a wife and kids, which wasn't going to happen—no way, no how—but clearly he had been focused on work too long if he'd forgotten how to talk to a beautiful woman.

He stepped into the elevator, tempted by her strawberry scent. He leaned forward at the same time she did, their fingers connecting as they hit the keypad, and Zach swore the spark of attraction lit up the plastic number and shot the elevator car off the ground.

An answering spark flared in her green eyes, revealing she felt it, too. And that might have been enough. Enough for him to consider pursuing the fascinating woman in front of him despite the half a dozen presentations he was working on, not to mention the promotion he was up for.

But then he noticed the floor she'd selected, that the meeting of their hands hadn't been due to fate but because they'd both reached for the same button. A bad feeling seemed to slow the elevator, pulling Zach back down to earth. "You're going to the fourth floor?" he asked. "To Knox Security?"

"Yeah, today's my first day on the job." Her green eyes brightened even more. "Hey, does this mean we'll be working together?"

That was, in fact, what it meant and should have been the end of his attraction. Zach never had and never would enter into a relationship at work. Too many pitfalls, too many complications, too big of a chance that management would think he had his mind on something other than the job.

Unfortunately, Zach hadn't forgotten that first smile, that first touch…

She's never let me forget, he thought with an accusing glance at the woman sitting in his passenger seat.

Not that Allison had gone out of her way to remind him of their first meeting or that instant spark of attraction. She didn't have to. Just the sound of her laughter drifting down the hall made his gut clench and sent another electric rush of the energy he'd felt at that first touch charging through his veins.

And every time she smiled at him, the flash of that dimple reminded him of his weakness where she was concerned, reminded him she was a woman who could do what no other woman had ever done—take his mind off his career.

He couldn't let that happen. His own childhood was a harsh reminder of what happened to a man who let a woman—who let *love*—break his focus. Zach would not repeat his father's mistakes.

So why on earth had he asked for Allison's help?

Because she's the only one who can do the job. And as long as he kept thinking of the dinner as part of the job, he just might make it through the night.

"When is Martha coming back anyway?" The sooner Allison left, the better as far as Zach was concerned. He'd forget all about her the moment she moved on to some other temp job.

"Monday. I'm coming in for another day or two just to catch her up."

"Good. That she's feeling better and ready to come back to work, I mean."

"Yeah." Something in Allison's agreement had Zach wondering if she wasn't as glad to be moving on. If there was some reason she wanted to stay...

"Have you ever thought of staying on some place? Not at Knox—" *please, not at Knox* "—but at some other company? A permanent position might give you the opportunity to work your way up—"

"No," Allison cut him off abruptly. As if realizing she might have given too much away, she flashed a smile and said, "Corporate ladders aren't for me. Afraid of heights. And I like the temp jobs. Moving from place to place, meeting new people... It's a good way to make sure I don't get bored."

Everything Allison said sounded legitimate, but Zach wasn't buying it. Who wouldn't want the chance to move up? To succeed? For Zach that need was a relentless drive that fueled him, pounding through his veins. Like the footfalls of another sprinter pulling away, Zach lived with the fear of not keeping pace, of falling behind, of failing...

But he was going to close the distance this time. He'd seal the Collins deal, if not tonight, then in another few days. Winning the bid would give him the edge over Bob Henderson when it came to the VP of Sales position both men were up for. Zach was sure of it, and he wouldn't let a complication like the flirtatious Riana Collins get in his way.

But as Allison shifted in the passenger seat, crossing her legs beneath the hint of lace at the hem of her skirt and drawing his attention to her slender calf and smooth skin, Zach feared his solution might prove far more dangerous than the problem.

"You're having your meeting *here?*"

Zach couldn't blame Allison for sounding more than a little incredulous as he pulled into the jazz club parking lot. "The location changed when James couldn't make it," he said wryly.

Later that evening, the place would be packed with people sipping martinis and listening to the blues. But six o'clock was too early for that crowd and perfect for an intimate dinner for two.

Maybe that was why his brain short-circuited as he climbed out of the car and circled around to open Allison's door. Surprise lit her eyes, and he swore silently. What did he think he was doing? He'd brought Allison along to remind Riana their relationship was strictly business, but who was going to remind Zach of that fact when it came to Allison?

I don't need any reminders. It was a momentary slip, he insisted even as her strawberry scent enticed him to fall even farther.

Taking his eye off the ball.

That was how his father would have phrased it, and Nathan Wilder knew how costly even a *momentary slip* could be. Nathan had been a high school star, starting quarterback with a promising college career ahead of him when he took his eye off the ball. When he made the *mistake* of getting his girlfriend pregnant. The echo of Nathan Wilder's voice, jag-

ged and sharp thanks to those broken dreams, sliced through
Zach's thoughts.

Could've had it all...

Nathan might not have been much of a father, but he had
taught Zach lessons he refused to forget. He didn't make mistakes. He wouldn't let anyone get in the way of the goals he'd
set for himself—not Riana Collins's unwanted attention and
certainly not his own equally unwanted interest in Allison
Warner.

Hoping to cover the too-personal act, Zach immediately
launched into a history of Collins Jewelers—the high-end
stores in Chicago and New York. The A-list celebrities who
wore the designs to red carpet events. The attention handling
the account would garner Knox Security.

He didn't mention his own goal for winning the account—
gaining the edge he would need to convince the board he was
the right man for the VP of Sales position.

In his hurry to get his thoughts back on track, he hadn't
realized he was half a step ahead of Allison until she mumbled something he didn't quite catch. Slowing until she fell
in step beside him, he asked, "What was that?"

"Everyone at Knox has been talking about this deal so..."
Her voice trailed off, and she shrugged as if making an embarrassed confession. "I went online and did some research."

Zach stopped short. "You did?"

The extra work showed an initiative Zach hadn't expected.
Allison was a short-term temp, filling in as a receptionist.
She smiled and laughed, made their clients feel welcome and
drove him to distraction. She answered phones, transferred
calls, and offered coffee until the meetings started and the
real work began. She said herself she had no ambition to move
up, only a desire to move on, so why would she take the time
to research one of Knox's potential clients when she'd be out
the door before he signed the contract?

"I ran James Collins through a search engine or two," she said almost defensively. "But it's not like that's going to help tonight."

"Right. Going into a business meeting prepared isn't the least bit useful."

Allison's eyebrows rose in challenge. "Well, it certainly isn't why you asked me to come."

After the shock he'd failed to hide, there was little point arguing otherwise. And she was right. He hadn't asked her to tag along because of her brilliant mind. He'd hoped Allison's presence might dissuade Riana, but deep down, he also had a backup plan. One he really hadn't thought he would need, so he'd ignored just how risky it might be. Kind of like being on a cruise and knowing those flotation vests lined the ship's railing in case of an emergency, but really...how many people gave a second thought to having to use one?

No one did. Not until the ship started to go under.

And with the look in Allison's eyes and the awareness eddying around them, drawing them closer with each pass, Zach could definitely feel himself starting to sink. All before he'd even put his suddenly dubious plan into motion.

"So what *exactly* are you expecting from me?"

If a third wheel wasn't enough to dissuade Riana, he'd thought he might hint his relationship with Allison wasn't strictly business. But what had seemed like a solid plan less than an hour ago now seemed much more like navigating through stormy, turbulent seas than smooth sailing.

"Like you said, I need someone to run interference."

"Okay, but who am I supposed to be?"

"You're not supposed to be anyone, Allie." He didn't know what it was about the use of the nickname that curved her lips into a small smile, but he could have kicked himself for using it. *Allison. Her name's Allison.* He didn't need to add to a sense of familiarity by giving her a nickname. He'd be better off calling her Ms. Warner. "You're a business associate."

Her dark blond brows rose higher, more eloquent and expressive than any long-winded argument could be. If he didn't know better, he'd swear she read his mind and... "You're enjoying this, aren't you?" He stepped closer to move out of the way of another couple headed for the door.

Dressed in business attire with their arms linked together, the woman's head on the man's shoulder, the pair appeared to be doing exactly what he and Allison *were not doing*—slipping away after work for a romantic rendezvous.

Allison glanced at the couple with one of those looks that women get at the end of romantic movies, all misty-eyed and sappy, like happily-ever-after actually occurred in real life. But then she looked back at him, and Zach wondered if he'd only imagined the moment. Her gaze sharpened to a needle-fine point, perfect for pinning him to a board and...

"What? Enjoying watching you squirm? Just a little," she said with a smile that said more than a little. "But do you really think my being here will have any effect on Riana Collins as long as she believes it's strictly business between us?"

Zach was right. She was enjoying this too much, but Allison couldn't seem to help herself. She knew, of course, anything this fun couldn't possibly be good for her and might end up biting her in the end, but she couldn't see how. After all, she had two, maybe three days left working with Zach. She'd move on to her next temp job, and Zach would still be at Knox Security, reaching higher than ever.

So what harm could a not-to-be-missed fantasy of dating Zach Wilder do?

Allison had her answer a second later when Zach's glower changed into something less dark yet even more dangerous. "You're right. Riana isn't the type to accept a subtle brush-off, and she knows I'm not the kind of man who mixes business with pleasure," he admitted. His voice lowered to a murmur that did more than heat up Allison's thoughts as he leaned closer and added, "But working with you, day after day, I found myself holding my breath to catch the sound of your voice, making excuses to walk by your desk just to see you smile, and I knew it was only a matter of time before I could no longer resist...."

His words trailed into a silence filled with endless possibilities before he asked, "Is that something Riana might believe?"

Allison swallowed hard. "Um, yeah, that—" She cleared her throat. "That might be convincing."

She didn't know about Riana Collins, but for thirty seconds, Zach had *her* completely convinced! Even now, standing so close, the faint, tantalizing smell of his aftershave tempted her to move closer. To not just breathe in the scent from the air, but to seek it out on the warmth of his skin. Allison's pulse pounded in her ears like a bass line blaring through the speakers of a tricked out car. Her whole body should have been trembling from the reverberations. "So...I guess the only question now is how obvious do we need to be?"

His gaze dropped to her lips, and Allison unconsciously ran her tongue over her lower lip as if she could already taste Zach there. Kissing her wouldn't be subtle at all. Kissing her would be obvious, bold, unquestionable... It would also be unnecessary since Riana Collins was nowhere around. But with the thought already in her mind, her own focus drifted from the desire darkening Zach's eyes to his mouth.

What kind of kisser would he be? If his technique matched his personality, the kiss would be quick, to the point, no messing around. And yet somehow Allison doubted it. Although she'd never seen a more personal side to Zach, the skip in her pulse and quickening heartbeat told her he *knew* how to kiss.

"Allie…"

The rough murmur of her name brushed against her nerve endings. It didn't even matter that she'd hated the nickname ever since her sister had started calling her "Allie-cat" back in the second grade. Heart pounding, Allison waited for Zach to lower his head. She swayed slightly, drawn closer by an almost undeniable attraction.

"Zach?" The sultry female voice should have come from Allison, but words were frozen in her dry throat, and not since a bout with laryngitis a few years ago had her voice sounded that husky.

It took Zach a moment to focus on a point over Allison's shoulder. Only because she stood so close did she hear his disgruntled sigh. "Obvious," he muttered as he placed a hand on her shoulder and turned her around. "Very obvious."

Allison's eyes widened as she caught sight of the woman walking toward them. When Zach said Riana Collins wasn't used to hearing the word no, Allison had assumed that was because the heiress to the Collins jewelry empire was rich and spoiled. She hadn't expected the reason to be because the woman was completely irresistible.

Dressed in a vibrant red skirt and jacket that hugged her curves, Riana Collins looked like an exotic supermodel. Black hair fell to her shoulders in a razor-straight style that emphasized her high cheekbones, smoky eyes and full red lips. Diamonds glittered at her ears and wrist, silently if not subtly promoting the family business. As the woman drew closer, Allison realized that wasn't the only advertising the woman did. She'd seen Riana, draped in gemstones and little else, in ads for Collins Jewelers.

This was the woman Zach was turning down—all for the sake of a business deal.

If Allison didn't know better, she might have thought Zach was hardwired with all the emotion and passion of a computer's CPU. But there'd been those few, brief moments when she'd seen the flare of attraction in his eyes, the desire of a flesh-and-blood man.

There was no sign of that man now as he greeted the stunning brunette. "Riana." His voice couldn't have sounded more professional if it had been a prerecorded phone message. His expression was equally polite, yet remote despite the obvious come-on in the woman's gaze. "So good to see you."

"You, too, Zach." Smoke turned to ash when Riana looked at Allison. "I didn't realize you'd be bringing anyone tonight."

"I've mentioned how eager Knox is to do business with you and your father." Sliding his hand to the small of her back, Zach brought Allison forward. "Naturally, we've brought out our best."

Hoping Riana Collins didn't ask best what, since she doubted the title of Best Temporary Receptionist would impress the woman, Allison held out her hand. "Allison Warner. Pleased to meet you, Ms. Collins."

Riana Collins looked less than pleased, an expression that didn't change as they entered the restaurant and followed the hostess to a secluded table obviously meant for two. A third place was hastily set. Zach kept Allison at his side, pulling out the chair to his right.

She might have expected the other woman to have a better chance of holding his attention, seated directly across from him. But he never failed to meet Allison's gaze before glancing at Riana, just like he never missed an opportunity to rest his hand on the back of her chair or brush his fingers against hers on the table.

At first, Allison thought Zach had decided to be subtle after all, only to quickly realize how wrong she was. The hand on her shoulder could have been a casual, business-related touch—until his thumb stroked the skin along her collarbone. And while even that small gesture might have *seemed* subtle, the shiver that raced down her spine like a quake down a fault line was anything but.

Judging by Riana's narrowed gaze, the woman had picked up on the aftershock.

After the first few minutes of small talk, discussing the menu and giving their orders to the waiter, Zach turned his attention to business. Riana nodded in all the appropriate places as Zach explained the different security options Knox offered; she even asked an informed question or two.

But the other woman still had more than business on her mind, and Allison wasn't surprised when Riana pegged her with a sharp look and said, "You've been quiet, Allison. I'd be curious to hear your thoughts."

For a split second her mind went blank, and she felt Zach stiffen beside her, his tension practically telegraphing an unspoken command straight through her. *Do not screw this up. Do not screw this up.* The added pressure had panic rising up inside her, but then the information she'd copied, collated, stapled and punched started filtering back. She'd always had a good memory for details—a useful talent when she'd juggled clients for Barton/Mills and one that helped with jumping from temp job to temp job now.

"Knox handles security for some of the top businesses in the Valley." Names from the client list flashed through her memory—a high-end clothing boutique, a chain of furniture stores, an office complex not far from where the new Collins jewelry store would soon break ground.

"I've heard your latest ad campaign," Allison added. It was an occupational hazard she had yet to break, paying more attention to ads than shows on TV or songs on the radio. "You've been promoting Collins Jewelers as the fourth 'C,' as important as cut, color and clarity. You have a reputation for accepting only the best, and when it comes to security systems, Knox is the best there is."

For the first time all evening, Allison felt Zach relax at her side, and the glow of satisfaction burned brighter as she caught his almost imperceptible nod of approval.

Night had fallen by the time they left the restaurant, but Allison's smile could have lit the sky. Zach waited for Riana to drive off in her Jag before he said, "I owe you, big time."

Her smile grew wider, bringing out the dimple in her right cheek, but despite the Cheshire grin, she passed on the chance to gloat. "No you don't. It was fun."

Judging by the bounce in her step and her smile as they walk toward his car, Allison was telling the truth. She'd had fun. When was the last time—if ever—that he'd thought of work as 'fun?' It was a challenge to be met, a range of pinnacles to climb, each higher and harder than the last. But fun? And yet when Allison reached the passenger door and turned to face him, he felt a hint of an answering smile tug at his lips. He couldn't deny that certain aspects of the evening had been…enjoyable.

It had been way too easy to let his gaze lock on hers, to brush his fingers over the back of her hand in a too casual to be casual gesture, to acknowledge the attraction he'd worked the past two months to ignore. Problem was, he didn't know how he was supposed to go back to ignoring it, to putting those jolts of lightning back in the bottle. But maybe he didn't have to.

Allison only had two days left at Knox Security. After that, they'd no longer be coworkers. She'd move on to another temp job, and he—he had way too much on his mind to even think of a serious relationship.

Who says it has to be serious? his libido argued slyly as they climbed into his car. The energy and excitement in her smile worked its way under his skin, buzzing with an awareness of how long it had been since he'd pursued *any* kind of relationship with a woman. And after all, Allison was all about fun, the kind of woman who might be open to something less than serious.

"I still say I owe you," Zach said once he'd pulled the car out of the parking lot. "How did you know those details about Knox's client list?"

"A few days ago, I ran copies of the company's references for some sales packets. I was pretty sure I remembered most of the names...and well, the numbers were a bit of a guesstimate."

"A guesstimate?"

"Okay, more of a guess, but hey, it worked, right?"

Zach felt any hint of a smile wiped clean away. No wonder he worked alone. He couldn't risk his future success on someone else who might have "fun" guessing at facts and figures. What if Riana Collins had figured out that Allison was making up her information? Allison could have blown the whole deal.

And she could have refused to help at all, his conscience goaded. She'd bailed him out when he asked her to, so it was a little late to worry about her methods.

"Do you still think you owe me or have I negated that with my creative sales pitch?"

Zach glanced over, catching glimpses of Allison's face in the passing streetlights like watching a flickering black-and-white television set. Only there was nothing old-fashioned or quaint about Allison. She was bold, confident, a high-definition type of woman. "The evening was still a success, thanks to you."

"What kind of girlfriend would I be if I didn't help you out?"

What kind of girlfriend *would* she be? The kind to

understand when he worked late at night, when he cancelled plans on the weekend, when he overlooked personal milestones for another professional stepping-stone? Or would she expect more—more of his time, more of his attention, more than he could give? Automatically, his hand tightened on the wheel. "Allie…"

"Relax, Zach. I was just kidding. I know you don't do relationships."

"Right."

"You're all about work."

"I am…"

"You don't have time to for play."

"Well…"

"And you'd make a terrible boyfriend."

Allison made that statement as he pulled into the underground parking garage at Knox. He found a spot next to her car, a lime-green VW bug, and cut the engine. She sat angled toward him, clearly expecting him to agree with everything she'd just said.

Which, he thought as he climbed from the car, was exactly what a smart man would do. Because everything she said *was* true. And yet when he met Allison on the other side of the car, he heard himself ask, "Is that another guesstimate?"

A puzzled frown touched her features. "What?"

"You've had a lot to say without knowing the facts."

Allison's eyes widened as he drew closer. She looked far more worried now than she had when he confronted her about bending the truth at dinner. "Well…"

"After all, we've never been on a real date."

"Of course not."

"And we've never kissed."

"No, but—"

"Never slept together."

A soft blush lit her cheeks. "Obviously not."

She took a step back only to bump up against the car.

"And while I might be a *bad* boyfriend, there are some things I'm very good at."

He stepped closer, trapping her against the hood of the car, but Allison didn't try to escape. He moved slowly, giving her time to protest but not so slowly as to give himself time to wonder what the hell he thought he was doing. He lowered his head, his gaze on her softly parted lips, but there was something else...

That dimple, the one that teased him whenever she smiled. She wasn't smiling now, but Zach couldn't resist brushing his lips against the spot as if the heated touch might somehow bring out the tiny indentation. He followed the subtle curve of her cheekbone toward her ear and the tender skin below her jaw.

Allison's breath caught as her head tilted back. She whispered his name and Zach couldn't deny the plea in her voice or his own need to really kiss her. Giving in, he slanted his mouth over hers, her lips soft and yielding beneath his own. She tasted like the Cajun barbecue sauce she'd dipped her chicken skewers into at dinner, a mix of spices made hotter by their kiss, and he couldn't get enough. Allison raised her arms, but instead of pushing him away, she ran one hand through his hair while the other wrapped around his tie, pulling him closer...

Desire pulsed through his veins, and the hands he'd placed on Allison's hips drifted into more dangerous territory. He didn't know how far over the line they would have landed if not for the beep of a car alarm several rows away.

The sound rang like a wake-up call to Zach's common sense. He was in a parking lot with Allison pressed up against his car like a would-be hood ornament. And not just any parking lot, but the parking lot at work where any fellow employee or—worse—his boss could walk by.

Lifting his head, he sucked in a much needed breath. "Allison—"

"We have to stop," she said, ducking away before he had a chance to protest. Her skin was flushed, her lips swollen from his kiss, her chest rising and falling rapidly, and it took every bit of self-control Zach had not to pull her back into his arms. "I mean, this is crazy. We're at work! I only have a few days left here and…"

"A few days," Zach echoed when Allison's words trailed away.

"Yes. Tuesday is my last day." The awareness shining in her eyes revealed all they weren't saying.

In a few days, Allison would no longer be a Knox employee. All the red lights that had him pounding on the brakes a second ago suddenly turned green… "Allison, don't take this the wrong way, but I can't wait until you're gone."

Chapter Three

"You're here early."

Zach looked away from his computer screen as his boss, Daryl Evans, walked into his office. "It's almost seven."

Not early by Zach's way of thinking. Maybe it was being born and raised in Phoenix, but he'd always believed morning was the best part of the day. Except during the worst heat of the summer months, dawn offered crisp, refreshing air and the kiss of cool dew on the grass. Brief moments of respite before the scorching afternoons.

That was how he felt about arriving at the office during those early hours, too. He liked the peace and quiet before the chaos of the workday began. Once eight o'clock rolled around, the silence was broken by ringing phones, beeping computers, and the chatter of his fellow employees going about their jobs. He liked that part, too. The energy and the noise and the occasionally hectic atmosphere. But he needed the soothing quiet first. Kind of like enjoying a cup of herbal tea before taking a straight shot of espresso.

Lately, though, Daryl had a habit of dropping in. Not just in the mornings, but at various times throughout the week. And that kind of interruption Zach *didn't* like.

Daryl was a good man, but Zach worked best alone. He didn't need anyone checking up on him any more than he needed weekly status meetings or the slaps on the back so many of his fellow employees craved. He didn't need anyone to tell him how important a client was or to do his best on an imperative sales proposal. He knew; he had his own ambition and drive to answer to, and they were harder task-masters than any boss could ever be.

"Obviously, I'm not the only one ready to get a jump-start on the day," Zach pointed out.

"At least I went home last night."

"So did I."

"And stayed there how long before coming back to work? Don't bother to lie," Daryl warned. "I'll check the cameras if I have to—one of the benefits of working for a company that sells security systems."

Zach was tempted to find out if his boss really would check the security footage, but then he thought about what Daryl might see— Zach leaving the parking garage with Allison or worse, Zach returning to the parking garage and kissing Allison. And while Knox didn't have a policy against relationships in the work place, Zach had never been tempted to engage in an office romance. It hadn't been worth running the risk that his boss might think Zach had something other than work on his mind.

The truth definitely seemed like a better option. Or at least a limited version of the truth. "I left around five-thirty for a dinner meeting. Came back at around eight—" kissed Allison for a few minutes that could have easily gone on forever " —to go over the revised blueprints for that new office complex in Peoria. By the time I checked to see what time it was, it was almost midnight. I *did* go home, but I was too wired to get much sleep, so I came back around six."

"How did the meeting with James Collins go?"

"He had to cancel," Zach admitted. "But I met with Riana."

"I see."

The words were noncommittal, but Zach heard everything his boss wasn't saying. Riana might call for a meeting, but James made all the executive decisions. Until Zach could swing another meeting with the man himself, the coveted contract would remain out of reach. He knew it wouldn't be long before he hurdled his way past Riana's seductive road-blocks, but he was quickly running out of time and patience.

What were the odds that the biggest contact of his career would be up for bid only two weeks before the board made their decision about the biggest promotion of his career?

If he didn't get the Collins account...

Zach shook the thought away. *When* he got the Collins account, he'd be a shoo-in for the promotion.

"The cancer research benefit is tonight. Riana is on the planning committee for the event, and she assured me her father will be there." He hated black-tie events, and a crowded ballroom wouldn't be the place to press James Collins for a time and date to present his proposal for the new jewelry stores, but at least Zach would have another chance to meet the man face to face.

Daryl nodded as he glanced around the office.

"So, what's on your mind?" Zach asked, straight to the point and with the hope the other man would respond in kind.

The slow perusal of his office couldn't be anything but a stall tactic. The place hadn't changed since Zach moved in five years ago. The large wooden desk took up most of the space in the middle of the room with a file cabinet in one corner and a trailing philodendron on a plant stand in the other. The plant stayed alive as long as it had only because the cleaning people watered once a week.

No pictures, no mementos, no trophies adorned the beige walls. He kept his personal life—such as it was—separate from work and liked it that way.

Except for last night when the two had combined in an explosive kiss. He had to be crazy to even contemplate dating Allison, and yet he'd done more than think about it, hadn't he? His final comment the night before intimated he was ready and willing to start…something.

He'd never been one for relationships, at least nothing serious. His career came first, and he preferred women who felt the same drive to succeed as he did. And while Allison was as beautiful, as smart, as clever as any of the women he'd dated in the past, she didn't fit the "work first" mold. She didn't fit *any* mold, he'd come to realize the night before. She was adventurous rather than ambitious, more interested in grabbing hold of the moment than reaching toward the future. A woman who would always keep a man on his toes, always keep him interested—

"It's about the Collins proposal."

Daryl's comment snapped Zach's attention back where it should have been in the first place. What was wrong with him? He'd never had trouble keeping his mind off a woman when it mattered. *Never.* And he refused to let it happen now.

Meeting his boss's gaze, he said, "Riana said Knox is in the running for the contract based on our initial numbers. That's what got us through the door, but our proposal will be what slams it shut on the rest of the competition." And the board would have no choice but to offer him the promotion.

Silence followed his statement. Hardly a ringing endorsement from his boss. Not that Zach needed that kind of encouragement, but did Daryl really think he would blow this chance?

"You know how important this presentation is to me."

"It's important to the whole company, Zach," his boss shot back, reminding Zach of criticisms he'd heard before.

Not a team player.... Doesn't work well with others...

Damn right he didn't! He worked hard, and he wasn't about to let anyone else drag him down.

Still, he took a deep breath and said, "I know. But you don't have to worry. I've got this one."

Zach knew it wouldn't look good to get too cocky, but if he showed any kind of weakness, Daryl—for all his mild-mannered attitude and scholarly looks—would move in for the kill. He'd pull the Collins account out from beneath Zach before he could say—

"I think you need help this time."

"What?" Zach stood so quickly his chair rolled back and bounced off the wall behind him. Daryl hadn't taken the account away, but this was almost as bad. "You can't—" Zach checked the response when he saw the steely determination behind his boss's wire-rimmed glasses.

Starting over and trying for a reasonable tone despite the frustration pounding through his veins, he said, "Look, Daryl, this has been my baby from the beginning. I've spent months working on this. For another salesman to come in now—"

"I never said it had to be another salesperson. One of the sales assistants can work with you."

Zach swallowed a derisive snort. The wanna-be salesmen were just as bad, if not worse. Scheming and striving to get ahead, to get where *he* was!

"Or an administrative assistant, someone to help with the details of putting the presentation together," Daryl suggested when Zach didn't jump at the sales assistant idea.

An admin. He still didn't like it. He worked alone—always had, always would. But his boss wasn't backing down on this, and if he had to have someone looking over his shoulder, at least he wouldn't have to worry about them trying to take credit for all the hard work he'd already done.

"All right," he conceded. "If you think it will help."

"Great," Daryl announced with a broad smile as if he hadn't railroaded Zach into the idea. "I have the perfect person in mind. Allison Warner."

"Allie—Allison?" Zach choked out her name, grateful he hadn't sat back down yet, or he would have popped back up like something had bitten him in the ass. "But she's —"

"She's what?"

A half a dozen descriptions came to mind, none of them the least bit appropriate. "She's a temp. She's only working here another two days. After that, she's supposed to be..."

Available.

"Leaving," he finished weakly.

"I know. It's perfect timing. Martha will be back, so we won't need Allison as a receptionist anymore. From what she's said, she doesn't have another temp assignment yet, so I'm sure she'll be eager to stay on. It's a chance for advancement that could lead to a permanent position here."

Permanent. Sweat broke out on the back of Zach's neck at the thought of seeing Allison day after day. The past two months had been bad enough, and that was before he'd kissed her.

How was he supposed to work with her now that he knew the softness of her skin? The taste of her kiss?

He'd deal with it, Zach thought grimly. He'd never had trouble focusing on work before and that wouldn't change, even if it meant working with Allison Warner.

I can't wait until you're gone.

The line might not have been the most romantic Allison had ever heard, yet every time Zach's voice echoed in her thoughts, tiny quivers seemed to shoot out along every nerve ending. She couldn't hear the words without picturing the intensity in his gaze or remembering the hunger in his touch. She'd been right about one thing—Zach Wilder certainly knew how to kiss.

He'd surprised her by starting with an almost innocent touch. But it wasn't just any kiss on the cheek. It was like those ridiculously small, bite-sized candy bars. One was supposed to satisfy a sweet craving, yet only left her wanting more, more, more.

But the question was, had she been wrong about everything else? She'd been so sure that Zach was an all work, all the time kind of guy. Yet he'd been the one to suggest...what, exactly? A relationship? Or merely the chance to finish what they'd started in the parking garage?

Allison didn't know. Like a refrain from a long-forgotten song—she couldn't remember the rest of the verses, so that one line kept playing over and over and over again. Even though it was killing her that she'd have to wait to find the answer, she respected Zach's decision. After the complete personal and professional disaster that was her ex-boyfriend, the last thing Allison wanted was an office romance.

So, it was with the hope that the next few days would fly by that Allison walked into the office Friday morning. As she slid her purse into the desk drawer, a masculine voice called out, "Hey, Allison. Daryl wants to see you in his office."

She glanced over her shoulder with a puzzled frown. "Why would he want to see me?"

Brett Mitchell, one of Knox's sales assistants, grinned. "Who wouldn't want to see you? Always makes my day."

"Hmm, you try kissing up to Martha like that?"

"Are you kidding?" Brett gave a mock shiver. "That woman is scary."

"You only say that because she can see right through your act. You can't charm everyone all the time."

"Ouch. That hurts, especially since I plan on making a career based on my charm," he said with a wink as he backed down the hall.

Allison shook her head at the younger man's antics, but her smile fell away as she considered the message he'd relayed. Why would Daryl Evans ask to see her? Before taking leave for her surgery, Martha had introduced Allison to Knox's division president. With his wire-rimmed glasses and his brown hair graying slightly at the temples, he'd reminded Allison of a college professor. He smiled at her in the mornings and asked for things like coffee and files and copies rather than demanding them, which was nice and not always the case.

But beyond transferring calls, setting up video conferences and handling some light administrative tasks, she'd had little contact with Daryl. Certainly nothing that merited a closed-door meeting. Maybe he just wanted to say goodbye and wish her luck on her next job. Despite the positive thought, Allison's steps slowed on the patterned carpet as she walked down the corridor to his office. While she didn't technically work for Knox Security, a performance review would be turned in to the temp agency. Those reviews had always been favorable in the past, and Allison had expected this one to be as well until now.

She'd done a good job, hadn't made any major mistakes… until she kissed Zach Wilder last night. Was that the reason? Had someone seen them in the parking garage? Heat crept to her face at the thought of someone having witnessed that kiss.

But it had been after eight by the time Zach dropped her at her car. No one would have been around that late. The meeting had to be about something else. Convinced of that, Allison gave Daryl Evans's door a quick knock and walked inside.

"Good morning, Daryl. Brett said—"

Her words lodged in her throat. Zach stood across from

Daryl's desk, a frown on his too handsome face. Certainty crashed into a world of doubt. "Zach..."

His well-controlled nod didn't do much to ease her nerves. "Allison."

Searching his gaze, Allison didn't know what she was looking for, but she knew she didn't find it in the remote, *businesslike* mask he wore. Any sign of the man who'd kissed her last night was completely gone. She should have expected it, but the loss hit harder than anticipated, like something incredible had just slipped though her hands. Which was crazy. She barely knew Zach. Her feelings were nothing more than a silly crush, and she'd have no trouble letting go.

None at all.

"Brett said you wanted to see me."

"Have a seat."

As Allison sank into the soft chair, she realized Zach must have sat there only moments earlier. The leather cushion still held the heat from his body, a warmth that enveloped her along with the hint of Zach's aftershave. The combination had her body playing tricks on her—her lips started to tingle, her stomach muscles trembled, and her bones threatened to melt into a weak puddle.

A movement from the corner of her eye caught her attention. Zach, crossing his arms over his chest. Zach, strong, solid, irretractable...

The memory of another meeting she'd walked into—ignorant and blind—crowded her thoughts until she felt claustrophobic, trapped in her own skin. Allison sucked in a deep gulp of air and forced the memory of Kevin aside until she once again had room to breathe, to think.

Let it go. Just...forget all about it. All of it.

If her time in New York taught her anything, it was to hold her head high even in the worst of situations. She hammered some steel back into her spine and sat up straight, ready to face whatever this meeting held in store. But even with her gaze fixed intently on her boss, her peripheral vision was suddenly twenty-twenty. She could see the cool blue of Zach's shirt, the tanned, leanly muscled forearms revealed by the rolled up cuffs, the narrow black leather belt around his flat abs, the crisp cut to the long line of his slate gray trousers.

She could even see the tension working his jaw and feel it coming off him in waves. Not so different from the masculine energy he'd barely held in check when she broke away from their kiss…

"Tuesday is your last day under contract with Knox Security."

Allison started at Daryl's words. "Yes, that's right."

He leaned back in his chair and studied her from across the polished expanse of his cherry desk. "You'll be pleased to know that Knox has extended that contract. Not as our receptionist, though. This will be a step up."

A step up. How could Daryl know she'd taken the short-term temp jobs as a way to avoid stepping up? She didn't want to climb the corporate ladder again. She'd learned the hard way that the higher you rise, the farther you fall. "Daryl, thank you. But—"

"You'll do fine," he reassured her with a fatherly smile that sent an ache to her heart.

But the pain only reminded her why she couldn't say yes. She'd already sacrificed too much of her personal life to the quest for business success. "I can't. Really."

"Of course you can." He slid a folder across the desk toward her. "I've already cleared it through your agency. You can handle this, Allison."

The confidence in his voice sent guilt worming its way beneath her skin. She did the job she was paid to do and liked to think she did it well. So why did she still feel like a trouble-making kid if she hadn't done anything wrong? But maybe that was the problem. Maybe her guilt wasn't in something she'd done. Perhaps it laid in all she *hadn't* done. To borrow a motto from the armed forces, she wasn't exactly being all she could be.

"This assistant position is perfect for you," Daryl added with a glance over her shoulder at Zach.

Assistant.

Realization formed a knot in her stomach as Daryl's words and Zach's presence sank in. Work...with Zach. How was she supposed to work with him day after day when her skin tingled with anticipation whenever he was near?

"Don't you agree, Zach?"

The firmly worded question told Allison that Zach had already made his *disagreement* perfectly clear. But his response was as cool and slick as the crystal on the face of the watch he wore as he said, "Of course. Allison will make the perfect partner. I'm looking forward to the start of our professional relationship."

Professional relationship.

As they walked out of Daryl's office together, Allison didn't need any special app from Zach's cutting-edge phone to translate what those words meant. The worst part was she should have seen it coming. She couldn't have anticipated Daryl extending her contract, but she had worked at Knox long enough to know Zach's reputation. Work first. Period.

Yesterday going to dinner as Zach's *girlfriend* had seemed like an adventure, one night of pretend before the clock struck midnight. But as with a different fairy tale, it was the kiss that broke the spell—a kiss that changed the moment from a fun adventure to something...more.

A kiss that had knocked down the protective barriers she'd built since the breakup with Kevin. One that overwhelmed her common sense and made her long to surrender her entire body and soul. And one that Zach regretted just as deeply.

Remember Plan A...

In a few weeks, she'd walk away from Knox Security—and Zach—without a look back. Whatever ridiculous hope she'd had that he was different from Kevin had withered at his frigid reaction in front of their boss. She wouldn't give Zach another thought. Not one...

"Allison, wait."

She turned at the sound of his voice, but he was closer than she thought. She took a stumbling step back to avoid running straight into his chest. He reached out to steady her, his hands bracketing her waist exactly like they had before he kissed her. Heat soaked into her skin from his touch, and Zach must have felt it, too. He snatched his hands back before they could burn.

"Allie—" He gave his head a quick shake. "Allison."

"Might as well call me Ms. Warner," she muttered.

He blinked as if the idea had actually crossed his mind. "What?"

"Nothing."

Silence fell between them, tension-filled and rife with *could have been* and *never was*. Zach sighed, regret flashing for an instant in his blue eyes. But then he straightened his shoulders, and his business-only mask fell into place. "I've been a salesman here for five years and not once has Daryl said I need help with a client. For him to insist on it..." The line etched between Zach's brows clearly spoke his displeasure with his boss's change in tactics. He shook his head. "I feel like I'm under a microscope right now, and I can't do anything that might be seen as losing my head."

And why did that make everything so much worse? To know she wasn't the only one who'd lost her head? It was one thing to feel control slip away during a heated kiss, but to hear him admit it as part of an argument for why that one kiss would never be anything more...

"Last night was a mistake. The best thing for both of us is to pretend it never happened."

Allison felt her face start to heat as anger burned inside her. Zach expected her to keep her mouth shut and go on with business as usual. Just like Kevin had. And while she could no way compare her long-time relationship with Kevin to a single kiss from Zach or his brush-off to Kevin's betrayal, Allison refused to make things *that* easy on him.

"It's too bad," she said finally.

"What is?"

"That we didn't know sooner that we'd be working together."

"I know. I'm glad we're seeing this the same way," he said, his voice grim, but Allison shook her head.

"I don't think we do. See, if you'd known we'd be working together, you never would have kissed me. Because now you're going to forget that kiss ever happened."

"And what would you have done?" Zach asked, the words sounding pried from his throat with a rusty crowbar. "Had you known we'd be working together?"

"Me?" She shrugged. "I still would have kissed you. But I would have tried a lot harder to make sure you *couldn't* forget."

It was the perfect parting shot, and had life been a movie with Allison in the lead role, she would have gotten away with tossing the line over her shoulder on route to the elevator. But life wasn't a movie, and she was starting to realize her sense of timing stunk. Instead of the director calling "cut," the crack of Daryl's door opening broke the moment, and both Allison and Zach froze. For a split second, her gaze stayed locked with Zach's before she looked over to their boss framed by the doorway.

"Good, you're both still here." Nothing in their boss's expression gave any indication he'd picked up on the tension between her and Zach, but Allison's sigh of relief was short-lived. "Zach, about that cancer benefit—take Allison with you. Your partnership starts tonight."

Chapter Four

It's only one night.

Zach repeated the mantra as he handed the valet the keys to his car. The refrain had been playing through his mind from the moment Daryl insisted Zach take Allison along to the gala at the upscale Scottsdale hotel. Lights glowed from inside and out, illuminating the lobby and the well-dressed men and women making their way through the frosted glass doors.

Just one night. He took a deep breath as he circled to the passenger side of the car and steadfastly ignored his conscience's biting reminder that he'd used that same justification the night before—a decision that could potentially make tonight and the next few weeks feel like tap dancing through a minefield.

Juggling a fake girlfriend and temporary assistant all wrapped up in one smart, sassy package would be difficult at any time. But to manage it when his total attention should be focused on winning the Collins account and making his case for the upcoming promotion...

He could do it. He *had* to. Zach refused to let this opportunity slip by. He wasn't going to spend his life looking back at his failures. He'd learned all he needed to know about could-have-beens from his father.

Nathan Wilder had been a dreamer. But instead of dreaming about a glorious future, his dreams had remained locked in the past. He was the high school golden boy who'd never eclipsed his popularity as the starting quarterback, a grown man whose crowning achievement in life was being named homecoming king his senior year.

Could have ridden that university football scholarship straight to the pros...

Could have made a fortune in endorsements.

And even as a young boy, Zach had understood why those could-have-beens never turned into more than that.

Could have had it all...but then your mother got pregnant with you...

Zach was the reason behind his father's life of failure. He had known that ugly truth since he was a kid, but he still got a sick feeling in his stomach whenever he thought about it. He'd seen old videotapes of the championship game where his father quarterbacked his team to victory. Nathan Wilder often watched the old games after he'd been drinking. Zach had come to despise football, but he'd seen those taped games as a kid. His father had been a great quarterback.

There was no telling what his father might have accomplished if he hadn't been burdened with a child he didn't want and a wife he'd felt obligated to marry.

It was a mistake Zach wouldn't repeat.

He was going to have his success, and no one, *no one* would be to blame because he would not fail.

All he had to do was keep his focus on his goal, to keep reaching for what he really wanted—

The passenger door opened, and Zach caught another glimpse of the long legs and smooth skin that had tempted him from the moment Allison opened her front door. Desire hit like a blow beneath the belt, sucking the air from his lungs and sending his blood rushing from his head. He should have been prepared, but he already had the uneasy feeling Allison was one woman who would always catch him off guard.

Her green eyes glowed, the dimple in her cheek on full display, as she held out her hand. "Have I mentioned how much I'm looking forward to this?"

"Several times," he said dryly even as he steeled himself for the warm, silken feel of her skin against his own as he led the way inside the hotel.

Anyone who thought revenge was best served cold never met a dish like Allison, Zach decided. There was nothing cold about the woman at his side. Her halter-style dress hugged the curves of her breasts and narrow waist before flaring over her hips and cascading in tiers to below her knees. Zach didn't know enough about women's fashions to name what the dress was made of, but the material had an iridescent sheen and captured all the warmth of a desert sunset. In one moment, the dress was gold, then orange and pink and red.... And even though it had to be nothing more than a trick of the lobby's crystal chandeliers, he couldn't help thinking the shifting, undulating glow came not from the overhead light, but from a fire burning inside the woman herself.

The charity event had brought out the best and the brightest of Scottsdale society, but as they walked into the ballroom, Allison put them all to shame. A flickering flame amid a room full of moths. And even though he knew he was only going to end up burned, the beat of the blood in his veins urged him closer.

"Are we fighting?"

As Allison leaned close, he caught the strawberry scent of her shampoo along with a hint of a sexier perfume, the sweet and spicy combination a perfect blend for the woman herself. With her scent filling his head, it took a moment for the words to gel. "Fighting?"

"I figure we need some kind of cover story for the scowl on your face."

She smiled at a group of men near the bar as they passed by, and Zach figured his "scowl" just got even darker when he saw the subtle nudges and nods in her direction, the immediate straightening of spines and lift to their shoulders, putting masculine interest on display. Allison didn't seem to notice how their gazes roamed over her golden skin and slender curves, but Zach turned her toward him, making sure his body blocked their line of sight.

The protective instinct was more familiar than the sting of jealousy, but in the past, Zach had always justified those feelings as an occupational hazard. He sold high-tech security systems, that was his job, but he liked the idea of keeping people safe. With Allison, though, *he* was going to be the one who needed extra security to keep her from slipping past his defenses with her spirit and sass and an ability to roll with the punches that had already saved him from Riana Collins once.

"We're not fighting."

She gave him a patronizing pat on her arm. "It's all right. We can always kiss and make up later."

"We're not fighting," he stressed as he leaned closer to make his point. And there would be no kissing. Until the Collins deal was sealed, they had to maintain the pretense of dating for Riana's benefit. But that charade didn't extend beyond the ballroom, so Zach had no reason to think of the

ride home to Allison's condo, of the walk to her door, of a good-night kiss, or—heaven help him—an invitation inside.

And yet he could see those moments reflected in the darkening of her green eyes, hear the whispered invitation in the sudden catch in her breath, feel the sexual attraction pulsing between them…

But then someone bumped into Zach from behind with a muttered apology, and the moment was broken.

Allison blinked, shaking off the same sensual spell that had held him captive, and regained her earlier confidence. "Then at least *try* to look like you're enjoying yourself."

"I think you're enjoying this enough for the both of us," he muttered even as he attempted to relax and pull off a passable imitation of a smile.

Over the next half an hour, Allison seemed to go out of her way to prove his words true. She hummed along with a cover band playing in the background, tapping her foot with the beat of the drum. She went back and forth between items up for silent auction, a tiny frown between her brows, as if debating where to spend her last dollar. She listened with empathy and encouragement as guests at the benefit shared stories of courage and survival.

But unlike his smile, unlike their *relationship,* nothing in Allison's words or actions was staged or put on for show.

"Don't you two make such a gorgeous couple," a silver-haired matron said over the music and laughter filling the hotel's gold and ivory ballroom.

"That's what I always say," Allison replied as she and Zach joined the older woman and her balding husband at a buffet table loaded with rich and decadent desserts. She slanted Zach a glance guaranteed to make a man's mouth water with a different but equally decadent hunger. "Isn't it, darling?"

"You know, the pretend girlfriend thing is only for Riana's sake," he muttered as the older couple drifted toward a fountain overflowing with drizzling chocolate.

Allison offered a sassy smile as she selected a chocolate-covered strawberry and lifted it to her lips. "Turns out I'm something of a method actor. I need to stay in character."

It was payback, Zach knew, and he deserved it. He'd hoped—foolishly, he'd known that even as the inane sentiments were leaving his mouth—by announcing they should forget the kiss they'd shared, it would somehow make it so. The wave of a magic wand even though he'd stopped believing in fairy tales so long ago, he couldn't recall an innocent, wide-eyed time when he might have actually thought they could come true.

Reality was a kiss that still sizzled beneath his skin and a mandatory working relationship that could prove untenable if he wasn't careful. But after the subtle touches and secretive smiles as Allison expertly pushed his buttons, Zach wasn't feeling careful. He was ready to push back.

He closed his hand around her wrist, taking more pleasure than he probably should in the slight flare of surprise in her green eyes. Lifting the slender hand still holding the strawberry she'd just tasted to his own mouth, he murmured, "Funny thing about revenge... It cuts both ways."

He may as well have aimed the warning at himself, but he didn't bother to heed it. The sharp edge of desire sliced at the tight reins of his control as he took a bite of the strawberry. It was only imagination that he could taste the flavor of Allison's lips in the fruit's fresh, juicy flavor. But he didn't imagine the leap in her pulse beneath his fingers or the subtle hint of color staining her cheeks as he held her hand and gaze captive. Signs that while Allison may have been playing, she wasn't acting.

The attraction between them was real, potent...and nothing but trouble if he couldn't get it back under control.

A sudden screech of feedback made Allison jump, and she quickly pulled her hand from his. He should have been grateful for the interruption. But as he watched Allison set the unfinished strawberry aside and wipe her fingers on an ivory colored napkin, part of him resented the intrusion.

"Thank you all for coming this evening." Riana Collins stood on the small stage previously occupied by the four-piece cover band. Dressed in a low-cut black gown, her dark hair pulled high in a sleek ponytail that accentuated her exotic features, she looked comfortable and confident in the spotlight. And why not? From what he'd seen by the well-dressed crowd—laughing, talking and drinking champagne—the benefit was going to be a success.

"She looks amazing," Allison commented as Riana thanked her fellow committee members for their hard work before introducing the president of the charity.

Zach shot her a wry look. "Now that is a statement no wise man would touch with a ten-foot pole."

"Oh, come on, Zach. You're a guy. And anyone can see Riana Collins is a gorgeous woman. I don't expect—" Allison cut herself off abruptly. Maybe because this wasn't a real date and neither of them were supposed to have any expectations.

But something in her acceptance bugged him. "More assumptions, Allie?"

"What do you mean?" she asked, her expression a little uneasy as she met his gaze.

"You've already said you think I'd make a bad boyfriend. Now I'm an unfaithful one, too?"

"I didn't say that," she argued. "I wasn't even talking about you in particular."

He eyed her carefully. "So who was he? The guy you didn't expect to keep his eyes off beautiful women?"

"Old boyfriend. Old news," she insisted with a toss of her blond head.

Her eyes snapped with the spirit Zach was getting used to, and he was glad to see it. "I hope you dumped him."

"Not as fast as I should have."

"Let me guess. Not before his hands followed where his eyes shouldn't have been."

She gave a short laugh. "Something like that. But the truth is, I should thank Kevin. If not for what he did, I wouldn't be here now."

If that was the case, then maybe Zach owed good ole Kev his thanks as well. He'd caught more than a few eyes wandering Allison's way throughout the evening, looks he'd warned off with a pointed glare even as a proprietary feeling filled him. Knowing he had no right to that feeling didn't make a bit of difference.

When it came to work, he'd done—and would continue to do—what he had to in order to get ahead. His clients were typically wealthy businessmen who enjoyed the finer things in life and surrounded themselves with people they saw as equals. Peers. Members of their own class. So Zach had learned to play golf, to appreciate a fine cigar, to know the difference between a hundred dollar bottle of wine and the stuff that came from a box.

Still, designer suits, champagne and caviar were as far from his hand-me-down, beer and burger upbringing as he could possibly get, and he always felt like an imposter as he walked into these black-tie events. The wrong-side-of-the-tracks kid dreading the moment when someone would spot the poor boy who didn't belong.

But tonight, anyone paying him extra attention was doing so only because of the beautiful woman at his side.

And even though it hadn't been his idea or Allison's for that matter, Zach found himself oddly grateful and, hell, *proud* to have her as his date.

"So I hope everyone has a good time tonight," Riana was saying in closing her speech, "and don't forget to bid on the items up for auction."

Glancing at the crowd gathered around the auction table, Allison said, "Let's go take another look. I haven't bid on anything yet."

"Got money burning a hole in your purse?"

"Yeah, right," Allison scoffed. "I'm just glad tonight's tickets come out of *your* budget since I'm pretty sure I blew all I'm allowed to spend on sticky notes last week."

Zach laughed, feeling more relaxed than he ever had in this kind of crowd. "Well, let's pretend you don't have that costly habit. What would you bid on?"

He'd barely glanced at the items earlier, but he wondered what had caught Allison's eye. A trip to an exorbitantly expensive day spa? He knew plenty of women who enjoyed that kind of pampering, but he'd noticed Allison's nails were a natural shade of pink, bare of the thick, brightly painted acrylics some women preferred. Her jewelry was simple, too. A pair of small gold hoops and a locket she wore often enough against her golden skin for Zach to know it was a sentimental, not fashionable choice. The intricate pieces of jewelry Riana Collins had donated didn't seem like Allison's style.

"Maybe one of the vacations," Allison mused.

"Vacation," he echoed as he realized he couldn't remember the last time he'd taken one. Not that he minded. He wouldn't get any closer to reaching his goals if he purposely stayed away from work. And he'd been working since he was a teenager. Even before then, there'd never been money to go anywhere. Vacation meant staying at home, and just the thought of slouching in an easy chair, his eyes glazed as he stared at the television set, Scotch in hand, had Zach breaking out in a cold sweat.

Warming to the subject, Allison said, "I can't tell you how many road trips my family took when my sister and I were growing up. Sometimes, we'd plan them for weeks—where we'd go, where we'd stay, what we'd do. Other times, my dad would come home early on a Friday, announce we were hitting the road, and we'd be on the freeway within an hour. Drove my mom nuts!"

But not Allison. Even now, her eyes glowed with the memory of the last-minute adventure. Look how well she'd jumped into this situation with Riana. He couldn't think of too many women who would have handled themselves nearly as well. And none who would have actually *enjoyed* it.

"Where would you go?"

She laughed. "Oh, my gosh. When we were kids, that was the best part—he wouldn't even tell us until we got there. Of course, once my sister, Bethany, learned how to read, she had to ruin the fun by telling me if we were heading toward California or up north to Flagstaff. If it was California, that meant San Diego. We'd spend hours, combing the beach for the perfect seashell before asking our dad who found the best one. Shockingly, it always ended up as a tie." She rolled her eyes. "You know how dads are."

No, no he didn't. Not fathers like the one Allison described. Listening to her talk about growing up was as foreign to him as hearing stories from someone raised on a solar space station. Hard as it was to comprehend, unwanted curiosity dragged him further into Allison's sunny childhood. "And what about Flagstaff? What did you and your family do there?"

"Well, it depended on when we went. Sometimes we'd go in the summer to escape the heat down here, but my favorite time was in winter because then we got to play in the snow!

My mom swore I'd end up with frostbite, but I loved every second of rolling down hills and diving headfirst into snow banks. We had a blast!"

She shot him a knowing look. "But you wouldn't know anything about that, would you?"

Zach tensed. Did it show? Was there something about him, some stain from his childhood he still hadn't washed off?

"When was the last time you took time off work to have some fun?"

His shoulders lowered on a relieved exhale. "You think I don't know how to have fun?"

"I think you're a workaholic who's so focused on the brass ring that you're completely missing out on the ride."

A bit of the light in her expression died, and the note of certainty in her voice made him wonder. Not that he thought she was right, but why was she was so sure she was right? Could her words be the voice of experience?

"What did you miss?"

Her green eyes widened perceptibly, a dead giveaway, a second before she glanced away. "We were talking about you." When she looked back at him, her smile was tinged with an unexpected vulnerability. "So what's it going to be? The trip to San Diego. Long walks on the beach and a sunset cruise... or going up north to a remote cabin near the Grand Canyon? Relaxing days filled with nature walks and granola?"

He studied her a moment longer, sensing a loss she couldn't hide even as her gaze pleaded with him to play along. To stay on the surface where answers were easy instead of digging deeper for a painful truth. And that was fine with him. He liked things shallow, superficial... So why, when it came to Allison's secrets, was he tempted to go looking for more?

"Allie—"

"Oh, I don't think Zach's going to have time for vacations, Allison."

Zach glanced over as Riana Collins stepped up to the bidding table. She brushed her ponytail over her shoulder with a hand draped in diamonds. "Not if he wins the bid for our company's security contract."

If... Riana dangled the word like a carrot, and Zach knew he was supposed to bite. He'd realized from the first time they met Riana was the kind of woman who enjoyed keeping people—men, especially—on a string. Like putting on one of his designer suits or wasting a day on a round of golf, Zach had considered playing along something he had to do. But for the first time, that string was starting to feel more like a noose, pulling tighter and tighter. It wouldn't be long, he feared, before something snapped.

As if sensing the direction of his thoughts, Allison stepped closer and placed her hand on his arm. To Riana or anyone else watching, the touch likely looked proprietary, but Zach knew the subtle squeeze wasn't for Riana's sake. He didn't know how Allison did it. How her touch could soothe one kind of tension in his body while igniting another...

"Still, you have to make a bid, Zach," Allison insisted. "It's for charity."

That was the one argument Riana couldn't win, and Zach had to give her credit. Reaching over, she picked up a pen from the auction table and handed it to him. "Allison's right. Tonight is about raising money. So...beach or cabin?"

Neither option held much appeal until he pictured a bikini-clad Allison strolling by his side on that California beach, smelling of the warm sun, surf and coconut lotion. Or wrapped in his arms beneath a warm blanket in front of a dancing fire in some distant log cabin with nothing but the two of them around for miles.

"Zach?" Allison prompted when he let the moment and his imagination drift for too long. Their gazes met, connected, and even though it wasn't possible, Zach thought he could see a flicker of that fire reflected in her green eyes.

"Cabin," he decided. "With nothing but nature and silence all around." And even though he had no intention of going anywhere, Zach wrote down a high offer guaranteed to give him the winning bid.

"Good luck, Zach," Riana told him. "It'll be interesting to see if you get what you want."

He didn't need the pointed look she shot him to know she was talking about more than the auction, and he was relieved when a woman stepped forward to ask Riana about one of the pieces of jewelry up for bid.

"Thank you," he murmured to Allison.

He'd lowered his head to make sure Riana couldn't overhear, but ended up closer than he'd intended, his lips nearly brushing against her temple. She'd smoothed her hair back that night instead of styling the tousled layers to frame her face. He'd always preferred long hair, but now he wondered why when Allison's short style revealed the delicate curve of her ear, the angle of her jaw, and the long line of her neck. The tempting hint of spice filled his head, and he could picture Allison dabbing on just a touch of the perfume in that delicate hollow and fought the urge to move closer and closer still. To seek out more of the scent on her skin and to discover where the trail might lead... Along the pulse he could see fluttering at the side of her neck? Over her collarbone and down to the hollow between her breasts?

Her throat moved as she swallowed, but she met his gaze—and the desire he knew had to be burning there—head-on. "So you don't think I went too far?"

No, he was the only one at risk of that danger if he didn't get this attraction under control. "You handled it perfectly."

Just like he'd known she would... Despite her justified

anger the day before and her willingness to torture him tonight, he trusted her not to sabotage him with Riana Collins. The idea that he had that kind of trust in Allison—especially when it came to something as important as his career—would have knocked him on his ass if he took the time to consider it, so he shoved the thought from his head. "Better than I was about to."

Studying him with a worried frown as if knowing what a rarity it would be for him to lose his professional cool, Allison advised, "You need to relax."

Allison was right. He'd dealt with difficult clients before without coming close to losing his cool. The stress of the Collins proposal and the promotion hanging over his head was making him lose his focus. It couldn't be anything else.

As the evening went on, Zach thought he did a fairly good job of taking Allison's advice. Together they mingled with the other guests sampling hors d'oeuvres, savoring glasses of champagne and listening to the band. He was enjoying himself—and Allison's company—enough that every now and then, he actually forgot to keep an eye out for James Collins.

He turned his attention back to the stage when the president of the charity stepped up to microphone once more and asked for the crowd's attention. The murmur of voices gradually trailed off as she said, "I want to thank you all for coming tonight and for the generosity you've shown. Not to mention the cutthroat sense of competition I saw out there as you tried to outbid each other on the silent auction items." A laugh rippled through the guests. "The auction is now closed, and I have the winning bids in hand."

Zach could feel Allison's glance as they waited for the woman to announce the winner of the vacation he'd bid on. He still wasn't sure what had possessed him to make the bid. Trying to prove something to Riana or to Allison?

Okay, yes, he'd been curious about the fun-filled vacations Allison and her family had taken. But it wasn't the idea of going on vacation that had him so intrigued, Zach had to admit. It was the excitement, the glow in Allison's features as she spoke that made him wonder what he'd missed. What he was *missing*...

"And congratulations, Zach Wilder, for your winning bid on a weekend getaway to the Grand Canyon."

Zach managed a smile at the charity's president. "It's for a good cause," he murmured.

"And you're going to have a *great* time," Allison insisted. "Think about it—entire days away from the office with nothing to do but take the time to kick back and relax—"

"Yeah, right." He gave a scoffing laugh. "I've got way too much going on to even think about missing work. With the Collins presentation—"

"There will always be another presentation, Zach."

"Well, it's not like the Grand Canyon's going anywhere. I can see it anytime."

"Uh-huh, and exactly how many times *have* you seen it?"

"Okay, I've never been but—"

"But nothing! You're going on that vacation even if I have to—"

"Have to what?" he challenged, wanting to see how far Allison might go, even if it was only in words. Would she say that she'd go with him? That she would make sure he worked on nothing but relaxed *pursuits* for the entire week in that secluded mountain cabin?

Her lips parted but before she could answer, a former politician's booming voice carried across the ballroom. "Riana, dear, you look stunning as ever. The spitting image of your mother. I've been wanting to say so to your father, but I haven't seen him yet tonight."

"Oh, Roger, I'm afraid he's working. You understand...

A man in my father's position can't afford to take time off. That's how he became so successful in the first place, you know."

Zach bit back a curse. Riana didn't so much as glance his way, but her words were as much for Zach as the man she was speaking to. The subtle dig cut deep, right to the heart of his determination to succeed, to break free of his father's failure and regret. Sometimes he didn't think he'd ever shake off Nathan Wilder's legacy as if it were ingrained in his DNA or inherited, like the dark hair and blue eyes his father had passed on to his son.

"I'm sorry, Zach," Allison murmured, taking his arms and steering him away from Riana. All the earlier teasing was gone, the sympathy in her gaze genuine as she gazed up at him. "I know you were hoping to talk to James Collins."

"It's the reason I came tonight, but it looks like Riana is going to win this hand, too."

Allison glanced back at the other woman with a surprising amount of empathy. "Don't be so sure."

"Oh, come on. Riana knew all along her father wasn't coming. It's another case of him *canceling* last minute, just like dinner on Friday. She's playing a game."

"I overheard some people talking earlier. Her mother passed away from cancer. This isn't just another benefit for her. She may not show it, but this is very personal, and I'm sure she's hurt that her father isn't here." Seeing his doubt, she pressed. "How would you feel if your father didn't bother to show up at an event that means so much to you?"

Relieved. That was how Zach had always felt as a kid whenever his father refused to attend one of his school functions despite Caroline's pleas. Any feelings of disappointment at not having his father in the audience had been smothered by the criticism and negativity that surrounded his old man like a dense, deadly fog. Didn't matter what he was trying to do—school play, science project, talent show—Nathan Wilder's *fatherly* advice never changed. *Get your head out of the damn clouds. You'll never be good enough.*

"Zach, if you want to leave—"

"No." The answer burst out before he'd given thought to what he might say.

Allison's brows rose. "Up for another round with Riana already?"

That would be a logical reason for why he wanted to stay—to show the other woman James Collins's absence didn't matter. But Zach feared his motives weren't nearly so simple.

His father had only dreamed of being at an event like this—surrounded by the rich and in some cases famous. Earlier, Zach had seen a former quarterback being interviewed by the media. That was the life Nathan Wilder once imagined. A life having a wife and son had denied him. But no matter how many times his father had seen himself amid this kind of crowd, Zach knew damn well Nathan had never pictured his son there. Maybe the in-your-face burst of satisfaction should have made him feel guilty, but it didn't. And as the band started its second set, the strains of a power ballad filling the ballroom and Allison gazing up at him, leaving was the last thing on his mind.

Holding out an arm, he asked, "Isn't this our song?"

"We have a song?" she asked even as she took his hand.

"We do now."

It's only pretend.

Allison repeated the reminder as Zach led the way to the dance floor. All part of the charade for Riana Collins's benefit. But the moment Zach slid his arm around her waist and pulled her close, thoughts of the other woman evaporated like water on an Arizona sidewalk. Allison couldn't think beyond the warmth and strength of his body brushing against hers in time with the slow, seductive music. Each breath drew in more of his cologne until she could almost believe the faint scent, and not simple oxygen, was what she needed to live. The edges of the ballroom seemed to blur and disappear as the world narrowed to the circle of their arms.

"My father would never have believed I'd be the one wearing a designer suit or rubbing elbows with this kind of crowd."

Catching the past tense, Allison briefly closed her eyes as she realized she'd stumbled over a sensitive subject earlier. "I'm sorry, Zach. When did you lose him?"

"When I was fourteen."

"Just a kid," she murmured out loud. As an adult, her father's death had devastated her. She couldn't imagine how she'd have coped if she'd lost him as a teen.

"I grew up fast," Zach said almost defensively as if her sympathy might somehow undermine his tough-guy masculinity.

"I'm sure your father would be proud if he could see you now. "

"You think so?"

Zach's cynical murmur had Allison second-guessing the validity of her statement. What kind of man had his father been that Zach could still have such doubts all these years later? She didn't know, but she was one-hundred percent certain her next words were true. "He should be. And so should you. You've accomplished so much already."

Not enough...

Zach didn't say the words; he didn't have to. Relentless drive revved just beneath his skin, and like bracing her hands against a sports car's hood, she could practically feel the shift and surge of power where her palm rested against his chest. It was a feeling she remembered from her years in New York. The roller-coaster excitement of ups and lows, hits and misses was as familiar and dangerous as an addiction. It would be so easy to slip back into craving that high...

But it was her craving for *Zach* that worried her even more. She'd walked a fine line throughout the evening, teasing and flirting and dancing out of reach when the flames got too hot. But she was well aware of exactly where that line was at all times, and she was careful not to cross it, not to lose control. She'd teetered on the edge a few times, the desire in Zach's blue eyes sapping the strength from her legs and leaving her dizzy, but she pulled back in time.

It was all part of the game.

But this—this was different. The feeling of connection, of understanding, cut deeper than desire or sexual attraction, slicing through vital organs and coming way too close to her heart. She swallowed, stunned by how easily he could slip past her defenses.

As the song came to an end and the band switched tempo to an eighties pop number, Allison quickly slipped from Zach's arms. "I think I'll go, um, check my makeup."

She didn't wait for him to protest or to hear if he even bothered, but she could feel the pinprick of his gaze following her until she escaped from the ballroom.

Like everything else about the hotel, the ladies' room was elegantly appointed, opening to a small lounge area with a vanity and mirror. Since she'd ducked away as an excuse to escape Zach for a few moments, Allison took only a cursory glance at her hair and makeup. But she needed time to remember all the reasons why she'd pulled away, and that wasn't going to happen in the five seconds it took to touch up her lip gloss.

Bracing her palms against the marble top, she gazed into her own reflection and hoped she could talk some sense into herself. *He's wrong for you,* she mentally scolded the weakness sapping her willpower. *If push comes to shove, he'll throw you under the bus in a heartbeat.*

Just like Kevin had.

She'd worked so hard to show she hadn't simply gotten the job at the ad agency by being his girlfriend. She'd wanted to make him proud, to be sure not to embarrass him. And for all her hard work and consideration, he'd humiliated her, costing Allison her job and the respect of the coworkers she'd once considered friends.

She had new goals and dreams now, ones that had nothing to do with work or relationships outside of her immediate family. She was going to be an aunt in a little over a month, and she was determined to make some progress in repairing her relationship with her sister as well as to discover the reason behind Bethany and Gage's separation. She wouldn't let anything get in the way.

Confident she had her priorities in order and her hormones under control, Allison had already turned toward the door when she heard voices from further inside the restroom.

"So tell us more about this gorgeous guy you've been after. Shouldn't you have him wrapped around your finger by now?"

Allison didn't recognize the voice, but she remembered the tone. She'd had her share of frenemies in New York— supposed confidants who'd later delighted in her failure. She was reaching for the door, ready to sneak away when a second voice chimed in and froze her in her tracks.

"I thought you were going to make your move last night, Riana."

She should go. Quietly slip out now without the women inside any the wiser. But even with her hand on the doorknob, Allison couldn't make herself move.

"Oh, don't worry. I have everything under control."

"You sound pretty confident considering he brought a date tonight."

Go. Now. The words shouted in Allison's mind, but she still didn't move. Like when she was a kid and had to touch the stove just to see if it was hot, she couldn't stop herself from listening even though she was just as likely to get burned. "Believe me, she isn't someone I have to worry about. I know men like Zach. I know what he wants and better yet, we both know I can give it to him."

Riana couldn't possibly have realized Allison was listening but as she slipped away, the woman's words seemed meant for her ears alone. "What can Allison possibly have to offer him?"

Chapter Five

"I can't believe you talked me into buying so much stuff."

"Oh, come on, Bethany!" Sitting across the table from her older sister at a family-style restaurant, Allison laughed, the sound a little too bright, a little too loud. Trying too hard... But the Saturday morning shopping spree was the first time Bethany had agreed to do anything with Allison since she'd moved back and she felt like she had when they were kids. Little sister tagging along—*can I come, too? Please, please, please!*—oh, so grateful just to be included.

She would willingly take the blame—and foot the bill—for the entire morning.

"You *need* that stuff," she insisted as she speared a piece of hard-boiled egg from her salad. "Babies require a huge amount of accessories."

Bethany was still shaking her head as she flipped through the receipts. Three years apart in age, the sisters looked so much alike even total strangers had no doubt they were closely related. Always the more reserved of the two, Bethany wore her naturally blond hair in a simple bob layered to frame her face. She liked pastels and solid colors over Allison's more vibrant prints, and had taken to wearing even more conservative outfits in the late stages of pregnancy. "All this for one little baby."

"How was your doctor's appointment last week?" Allison asked as her sister finally set the receipts aside and turned to her own garden salad. "Did you have an ultrasound?"

"No, I already had one a while ago."

She stopped with a bite halfway to her mouth before setting the fork aside. "You already know what you're going to have?"

And you didn't bother to tell me?

Hurt stopped Allison's breath in her chest. She and Bethany had been so close once, sharing everything from clothes and shoes to their highest hopes and deepest secrets. But Allison didn't even know the sex of her sister's baby.

"No." Bethany shot her quick glance before she dropped her gaze back to her salad. "I didn't ask. I want it to be a surprise."

"Oh." Allison exhaled on a relieved sigh. "Sorry, I just—"

She bit off the words before she could complain about feeling left out. Not only would the words sound pathetically self-pitying, but her complaint would open the door for her sister to point out three years' worth of unreturned phone calls, missed holidays, and broken promises. Bethany might not have welcomed her back with open arms, but Allison had only herself to blame.

After a brief hesitation, Bethany reached into her purse, tucked beside her on the booth's red vinyl seat. "Here, take a look. I've been carrying this with me."

To Allison, the grainy photo looked like a snapshot taken of a television set that had lost reception. If not for the small, white arrow pointing to the baby's head, she wouldn't have had a clue what she was looking at. But what a difference that arrow made, transforming black and white nothingness into a living, breathing miracle.

"Oh, my gosh! You're having a baby!"

Bethany rubbed a hand over her extended stomach. "Yeah, I'd kind of figured that out already."

"I know, but look!" Allison stared at the ultrasound picture, the miracle of her niece or nephew. "Have you thought of names? Of course you have. Do you—"

"No, I haven't decided," Bethany insisted.

Allison set the ultrasound picture aside, knowing her sister's sudden reticence had more to do with her separation than it did with picking names for the child she carried. "Have you seen Gage?"

Bethany shook her head. The quick movement sent her chin-length hair swinging. "Not since he moved out."

Her sister still hadn't told her the reason for husband's abrupt desertion. Even though their mother believed Allison would be the one her sister would open up to, Allison knew she'd lost the right to ask. It would be up to Bethany to tell her what had happened, and if she didn't, well, then it would be up to Allison to keep her questions at bay.

The silent separation reminded Allison of a rare fight back when they'd shared a room as kids. Bethany had walked off a line bisecting the area between their beds, an invisible barrier between the two of them. They were adults now, but Allison felt that emotional line and read signs in her sister's expression that clearly warned, "Do not cross."

Still, she had to ask, "You are happy about the baby, aren't you?"

Her sister picked up the black-and-white picture. A smile trembled on her lips as she rubbed her thumb across the image. "Of course I am. I've always wanted a baby. Always," she voice drifted away on a whisper. "But this isn't how I expected...things."

"I'm sure whatever problems you're having with Gage, the two of you will—"

"What about you?" Bethany asked suddenly, interrupting the encouragement Allison would have given.

"What do you mean?"

"How's work?"

Allison dropped her gaze to her salad, digging through the lettuce as if hunting for lost treasure. As kids, the sister had sworn they had a kind of sibling ESP when it came to reading the other's mind. Despite the distance between them, she feared her sister would end up reading her thoughts—not about work, but about Zach.

She wouldn't have thought it possible, but Allison owed Riana Collins. Overhearing the other woman's conversation had shored up Allison's defenses like no mental pep talk could. Success meant everything to Zach, and if he was going to cross the line from business to pleasure, didn't it make more sense for him to cross it with Riana? After all, he'd made no secret of how badly he wanted the Collins deal, and Riana had considerable influence over who might get it.

She could give Zach's career an extra boost while Allison would be little more than a speed bump along the way.

And yet when he'd walked her to her door last night, for a brief moment illuminated by her front porch light, she'd seen the desire in his eyes, felt the heat as his gaze locked on her lips, and knew he wanted to kiss her again. Maybe as badly as she'd wanted him to kiss her. But what did it mean that he was tempted to break his rules? That the sizzle of attraction between them was somehow special? Or was Zach simply the type to bend his beliefs to fit the situation?

Allison didn't know, and she feared it wasn't possible *to* know until it was too late to protect herself and she ended up

---

emotional roadkill once again. She was still dusting off from the last time and wasn't willing to take another chance. So she'd ducked away with Riana's voice ringing in her ears.

I know what Zach wants... We both know I can give it to him.

Allison had no illusions that she could make any such claim, but that didn't keep thoughts of seeing Zach, *working* with Zach, from circling around and around until she felt dizzy.

"Work is fine," she insisted, but her sister still picked up on her uncertainty even if not for the reason behind it.

Bethany gave a soft sound of disbelief. "Which means you're bored out of your mind."

"I never said that," Allison protested.

"You didn't have to. Anyone can see it."

Bethany spoke the words with an older sister certainty that had never failed to annoy Allison. She took a deep breath, determined not to fall into a battle of "am not" versus "are too." "See what? And how? You've never been interested in my work."

"No, but I know what you've been doing. Yoga on Monday, pottery on Tuesday, gym on Wednesday, arts and crafts at the community college on Thursday, book club on Friday—"

"Yeah, so I have a lot of interests," Allison said, somewhat defensively even as she refused to make excuses for her sudden acquisition of a dozen or so hobbies or her dismal failure at most of them.

"You have a lot of time because you have a job that doesn't hold your interest. Even if you don't want to admit it."

What Allison didn't want to admit was that she'd purposely left time open with the hope of using it to salvage her relationship with her sister, an effort that so far had proved as big a failure as her hobbies.

"I like the temp jobs," she insisted, "and, well, the one

I'm working now has turned out to be anything but boring."
She didn't know what working with Zach would be like, but
she wouldn't be bored. "Besides, I wanted to be around for
Mom. In case she needed me." Thinking of her mother, Allison added, "I hope she's having a good time."

Though it had been Donna's idea to cruise the Mexican
Riviera in memory of her late husband, Allison didn't think
her mother had ever traveled without her father. She'd certainly never left the country.

"Oh, she said she's having a great time."

"You talked to her? When?" Ship to shore calls cost a fortune, so Allison hadn't expected to hear from their mother
during the three weeks she was gone.

"Yesterday while the ship was in port in Cabo San Lucas.
She was only on shore for a few hours, so she called me to
check in. I'm sure she'll call you when she gets a chance. She
didn't want to bother you at work."

Bethany said the words casually, but for Allison, there was
nothing casual about them. Bethany turned her attention back
to her meal, but for Allison the bite of fresh bread had turned
to glue, sticking in her throat and refusing to budge. Callously
rubbing in the reminder of a missed phone call seemed too
cruel even if Bethany hadn't forgiven her, yet Allison couldn't
believe her sister had forgotten.

The last time Bethany had tried to get a hold of her at work
was with the news that their father had had a heart attack.
In the middle of an important advertising pitch, it had been
hours before Allison received the message. In the end, she
won the account—but lost her father.

Allison had to give Daryl Evans credit. When the man
made up his mind to make a move, he didn't wait. The origi-
nal plan had been for Allison to stay on hand at the reception
desk and help Martha ease back into working full time. But

by the end of the day on Monday, the older woman was eager to get back to her old job and all too willing to ease Allison into her new position as Zach's assistant, starting first thing Tuesday morning.

Someone from IT had already set her up with a laptop and Daryl had arranged for another desk to be added on to Zach's, creating an L-shaped workspace for the two of them. Martha had encouraged her to take the last hour of the day to arrange her new space to her liking, and Allison had transferred all her personal knickknacks from the receptionist's area to the office she would now share with Zach. She'd just perched on the edge of her chair when Martha's voice sounded over the intercom.

"Allison, there's a woman here to see Zach." Lowering her voice, she whispered, "She doesn't have an appointment."

"But he's not here." Allison hadn't seen him all day, but that hadn't stopped her heart from skipping a beat every time the elevator bell chimed.

"I tried to get her to reschedule a time later in the week," the receptionist was saying, "but she said she'd rather wait and that she'd be more comfortable in Zach's office."

Riana Collins. Zach might have dozens of clients, but those words couldn't have come from anyone else.

"Go ahead and send her back."

Allison took a deep breath and put on her best professional smile even though she doubted Riana's reasons for dropping by had anything to do with business. Her suspicions were confirmed when the other woman blinked in surprise as she spotted Allison. "I thought this was Zach's office."

Despite the frown tugging at her brows, the other woman was gorgeous as ever in a ruby red sweater and black skirt topped by a short flared trench coat in deference to the gray clouds that had blown in over the weekend and lingered all day. She looked ready for a photo shoot, and in her own seafoam sweater and beige skirt, Allison felt washed out by comparison. Not even the floral scarf she'd added to give the outfit an extra pop of color helped dismiss the feeling.

Still, she held her head high as she said, "It is. We share the space." She took a brief glance at the desks behind her, grateful Daryl had outfitted her role as Zach's assistant so quickly and slightly amused that, if anything, *Zach* appeared like the newcomer to the office. "Zach and I work very closely together, so if there's anything I can do—"

"I'll wait for Zach. I called him earlier, and he said he was on his way back. But in the meantime, we'll have a chance to talk."

Allison couldn't think of much she'd like to do less, but she kept her smile in place. "I hear the gala on Friday broke a record for donations. Congratulations."

"The evening was a success. Everyone who was there said so."

Riana tossed her head proudly, but the bravado didn't hide the hurt that Riana's own father hadn't been among the *everyone*. Allison felt a touch of sympathy for the other woman, but the feeling didn't last long as Riana continued, "I have to admit, I was surprised to see Zach with you."

"Why is that?"

"He doesn't seem the type to have an office romance, but then I suppose it's convenient, isn't it? With as much as Zach works, you probably wouldn't see him much if you didn't work together."

The cutting dig was effective; no woman wanted to be thought of as little more than a convenience, and Allison had to force herself to remember that she wasn't Zach's convenient girlfriend. She was his *pretend* girlfriend, and no matter what she'd told Zach about her method acting, there was no reason for Allison to feel a tug of anger as Riana tried to jerk her chain. No reason at all.

"Zach does work hard, but we make time to see each other. I guess you could say it's quality over quantity."

"Well, I hope you don't mind if that quantity takes a significant drop over the next few weeks."

"And why would that happen, Riana?"

Zach's deep voice struck a chord inside Allison that resonated throughout her body until her nerve endings started to sing. She turned toward the door and soaked in the sight of him, as if over the weekend she'd somehow forgotten how gorgeous he was. She hadn't, but she'd spent much of that time convincing herself his eyes weren't that blue, his dark hair that thick, his mouth that tempting, his features that perfect a combination of rugged and handsome. Time she'd wasted because Zach was all that and more.

Of course *more* in this case included unavailable, but knowing that didn't keep her pulse from pounding. He was dressed as impeccably as ever in shades of gray that carried from his tie to his trousers, but she could see signs of wear and tear showing through. From the creases in his forehead to the tiredness around his eyes, she was willing to bet he'd worked straight through the past three days. Sympathy tugged at her, reaching out and drawing her closer, even though those same telltale signs of a man addicted to his job should have sent her running.

"Because..." Riana drew the word out like a drum roll, "my father wants to see your proposal next Friday. I told him you wouldn't have a problem with that deadline."

Allison figured Zach wouldn't have had a problem if Riana had told him the meeting was tomorrow. He'd just kill himself to get it done on time. But she shoved her resentment at the other woman's game playing aside. This was what Zach wanted, what he'd worked so hard to achieve. And while Allison's goals may have changed, she hadn't forgotten the euphoria of a job well done.

But Zach hid whatever he was feeling behind a simple nod of his dark head. "Next Friday it is."

"You're also invited to a groundbreaking ceremony at our new site tomorrow."

"We'll be there."

Allison doubted Riana missed how Zach subtly included her in the invitation. Judging by the other woman's smile, Riana had not only expected but was anticipating her presence at the groundbreaking. "I'm looking forward to it."

Allison definitely couldn't say the same.

"I've been telling my father quite a bit about you, Zach, so I hope you don't disappoint."

The warning in her parting words was impossible to miss as Riana left the office, but Allison paid no attention. The excitement bubbling up inside propelled her forward with a bouncing half step, but she stopped shy of throwing herself into Zach's arms. A hug, even one intended as an innocent offer of congratulations, would be far too dangerous.

She'd thought she made the right decision on Friday, ducking away from the good-night kiss that almost happened, but somehow a kiss they hadn't shared was becoming almost impossible for her to ignore. The *what if* of the moment had gained strength, like a wave building and growing as it rushed toward the shoreline. That almost-kiss seemed just as inevitable, and when it finally hit, Allison doubted she'd have the will to resist the sensual undertow.

Even worse was the awareness in Zach's blue eyes as he checked her reaction, knowing she didn't trust herself to touch him. Hoping to cover up her susceptibility to him, Allison quickly said, "Congratulations, Zach. You did it."

"Don't open the champagne just yet. This is only the first step."

The first step in winning yet another account...and another...and another. The reminder of Zach's unrelenting drive and the reasons *why* she'd ducked away from his kiss should have sent any thoughts of what if into the deep freeze. But behind the fierce determination in Zach's straight shoulders and confident stride as he walked toward his desk and waiting computer, she could still sense that hint of vulnerability. The one she was sure he hadn't intended to reveal when he talked about his father.

My father would never have believed I'd be the one wearing a designer suit or rubbing elbows with this kind of crowd.

Was it any wonder he pushed himself so hard?

The smart thing would be to just let it go, to let Zach keep pushing himself the way he always had, the way he always would. She didn't really think she could change him, did she? Surely she wasn't *that* foolish. Walking over to the mini fridge in the corner of the office, Allison was starting to think she was that foolish and more. But it didn't stop her from pulling out two bottles of water and holding one in front of Zach's face. He looked away from the computer screen, eyebrows lifted in question.

"No champagne. Promise. Just thirty seconds to toast that first step."

His lips lifted in the faintly puzzled smile she was starting to recognize, but he took the bottle and twisted off the plastic cap. Tapping her bottle against his, Allison said, "To first steps."

"To first steps," he echoed.

But it wasn't business firsts crossing Allison's mind as he lifted the bottle to his lips. Instead first kisses, first dances and other more intimate firsts teased her senses. She took a sip of her own water, but it did little to quench the sudden heat rushing her cheeks as their gazes locked.

A knock against the doorframe broke the moment as Daryl stepped inside the office. "I hear congratulations are in order. I saw Riana Collins on her way out. She said you've got a meeting with James next week. Now aren't you glad you you'll have Allison here to help with the proposal?"

"I had a feeling Riana might spring a short deadline on us, so I pretty much have the whole thing done."

Daryl frowned but merely asked, "What do you have in mind for the presentation?"

"I have our recent sales figures already compiled as well as our customer service surveys. Once I see the actual blueprints, I'll give Collins every option he could ask for. I want to go in with the specs on our latest technology to start. Motion detectors for the showroom, pressure-sensitive alarms for the cases, cameras to cover every angle, and I'll work from there to give him everything he wants."

Daryl nodded thoughtfully as Zach continued, but Allison sensed their boss was waiting for something more. Only it turned out he didn't want that something more from Zach, but from her. Pinning her with a look from behind his wire frames, Daryl asked, "What do you think, Allison?"

"It's, um, a lot of information."

"That's okay," Zach insisted. "You haven't been here that long. You can't be expected to know everything about our systems."

"I suppose not," she agreed, knowing he was right and knowing, too, that he probably thought he was helping. Defending her even if he'd done it in a completely patronizing way. "I don't know nearly as much as you do about all this technology, but I'm guessing James Collins won't either. And you're giving him a lot of information without establishing a connection between Knox and Collins Jewelers."

"A connection?" he echoed. "I want to win another account, not make a love match on a game show."

She knew Zach wasn't the type to be open-minded to ideas other than his own, but Allison hadn't expected the immediate rejection of her opinion. And it hurt. Their "relationship" might have been nothing but show for Riana Collins, but after Friday night, Allison thought she'd done enough to genuinely earn Zach's respect. She'd been wrong. Again.

"You and every other security systems firm in town," she shot back. "What's to keep Collins Jewelers from simply being *another account?* Why should James Collins pick Knox?"

Zach opened his mouth to argue, Allison was sure, but Daryl beat him to it. "That's an interesting question, Allison, and I'm glad you mentioned it. It's always good to see things from a fresh angle."

Thinking he was about to brush off her idea only in a kinder, gentler way than Zach already had, Allison was un prepared when Daryl turned to Zach and said, "I think you need to pursue Allison's idea for the Collins proposal. Give it a personal twist."

A personal twist.

The only personal twisting going on was happening in Zach's gut after his boss spoke that last pronouncement and left. What the hell was Daryl thinking? Everything he'd read, and Zach had read *everything,* pointed to James Collins as a serious, no-nonsense businessman. Hadn't Allison been the one to recognize that James had been willing to risk disappointing his daughter by missing the benefit that should have meant a great deal to them both?

Something she should have remembered before she started talking about the best way to reach out and touch the man's feelings!

"Zach…"

"Do you realize my first meeting with James Collins was nearly a month ago? That I've been working on my presentation that whole time? And now I've got a week to do the whole thing over?"

Allison swallowed, but she didn't back down. "Daryl asked for my opinion. You don't have to agree with it—"

"No, I just have to rework my whole presentation around it."

"Daryl didn't say that. Only to give it a more personal slant. To make Collins feel like Knox is the right choice." Doubt must have been written on his face because Allison stepped forward, warming to the subject. "Think about it, Zach. Why does a forty-five-year-old man buy a sports car? Is it because those cars are safer or better made? Maybe. Are they five or six times better than a used sedan? Probably not. But that guy's willing to pay five or six times more to get that sports car. Because of the way it makes him feel. Rich, powerful, sexy..."

"Do not tell me I have to go into a meeting and make James Collins feel sexy."

A faint blush lit her cheeks and her lashes dropped to hide her eyes, but not before he saw the hint of desire flare in her eyes. Trying hard not to notice, he picked up on the hitch in her breathing, the quickening of the pulse at her throat. Music drifted through his memory, turning his mind back to Friday night and the warmth and softness of holding Allison...

His throat caught as he tried to swallow, his mouth suddenly dry, and he thought maybe Allison knew what she was talking about. She damn sure knew how to make *him* feel! As frustrated as he was by Allison's interference, he still wanted to pull her into his arms, to have her body pressed against him again.

"You need to make him feel *something,*" Allison stressed. "And I can help—"

"I don't need any help."

Added pressure of reworking his proposal on a shortened deadline aside, Zach fully intended to win the Collins account. But rise or fall, he would do it on his own. His success or his failure. He wasn't his father. He wouldn't keep someone around just to have a fall guy to blame if it all went wrong.

"That wasn't what you said last week."

"That was different."

"Different. Right." Allison couldn't keep the faintly mocking tone from her voice. Because last week all he'd needed her to do was smile and look pretty. Hadn't working with Kevin taught her all about that? He hadn't wanted her to have her own ideas either—especially not if they were going to be better than his.

Zach swore. "I didn't mean—"

"I think your meaning was perfectly clear. You—"

"Um, excuse me?"

The crackle of Martha's voice across the intercom froze the rest of Allison's words in her throat. She'd been too worked up to notice the phone's initial beep and hated to think what the older woman might have overheard. She hadn't even started her official first day, and already she and Zach couldn't talk to each other without arguing.

Even Zach looked a little embarrassed as he asked, "What is it, Martha?"

"There's a phone call."

"What line?"

"Line two, but it's for Allison. Her sister."

Bethany? Her sister rarely called her at home and *never* at work. Memories of the last time her sister had called her at the office flooded over Allison until she thought she might drown.

"Allison? Are you okay?"

She barely recognized the feel of Zach's hands at her shoulders or the concern in his blue eyes. "I have to— My sister—" Brushing by him, she grabbed the phone and instantly knew something was wrong. She could hear the clog of tears in her sister's voice. "Bethany?"

"I didn't want to bother you at work."

"Forget work. Tell me what's wrong."

"The delivery men came with the furniture."

"Okay." The words were the last she expected to hear but didn't slow her heart.

"I-I don't know what to do. When they said they delivered, I thought they meant they *delivered,* not that they'd just dump everything outside and—" Her voice cut off with a gasp followed by a loud thump.

"Bethany? What happened? What's going on?"

By now, Allison could tell the tears were no longer threatening. Her sister was crying as she said, "The wind just blew the crib over."

"The crib is outside?" Allison turned toward the window in Zach's office as if she could somehow see her sister's townhouse from there. Two days' worth of dark clouds were finally delivering the promised storm—a few scattered raindrops pelted the glass and the palms across the street waved wildly.

"*Everything's* outside. In *boxes!* The man said we only paid for delivery, not installation, and that we didn't tell them we needed them to carry everything upstairs to the townhouse."

Bethany's townhouse had a first-floor garage with a staircase leading to the kitchen and exterior stairs leading to the front door. "Well, tell them we'll pay the extra for second delivery and installation," Allison said as her breathing started to slow. This, this was a problem she could solve, a call for help she could handle. She already knew what she'd say to the salesman who hadn't mentioned an additional delivery or installation fee.

"I tried that, but they said because it wasn't on the schedule, they wouldn't have time."

Hearing the note of hysteria growing in her sister's voice, Allison kept her words firm and matter-of-fact. Giving in to sympathy would be the thing to push Bethany over the edge.

"Then they're going to have to take everything back to the store, and we'll reschedule the delivery for a day when they can actually deliver the baby furniture inside the house and put it together."

Silence filled the line, and Allison closed her eyes and rubbed her forehead, already knowing what was about to come. "They've already left," Bethany said in a small voice. "I didn't think—" A sob cut off her words. "How am I going to handle delivering a baby when I can't even handle a delivery of *furniture?*"

The connection was a bit of a stretch, but Allison knew that right now, everything in her sister's life revolved around her pregnancy and the coming baby. "You *can* do this, and when that baby comes, Mom and I will be there to help every step of the way. For now, sit tight. I'll be there in a few minutes, and we'll figure out what to do."

"O-Okay." Bethany sniffed and offered a quiet, "Thank you, Allison."

"Hey, what are sisters for?" she teased against the lump in her throat. The last thing she wanted was for her sister to stress out at a time like this, but Allison was grateful for any opportunity that might help bridge the distance between them.

The second she hung up the phone, she could no longer ignore the pinprick of awareness lifting the hairs on the back of her neck. And although she wasn't the least bit surprised to find Zach watching her, it *did* leave her feeling disconcerted to know she'd already become so attuned to his presence that she could sense the weight of his gaze.

"I have to go."

"Allison, wait."

Thinking he might try to stop her, she overrode his protest. "No. I think we've said all we have to say to each other right now, and unlike you, my sister *does* need my help."

"And you're going to do what? You can't move the furniture yourself."

Everything about Zach—from the muscular arms he'd cross over his broad chest, to his widespread stance, to the certainty in his blue gaze—spoke of strength, confidence and ability. It was almost impossible to imagine him needing someone or wanting to be needed. The emotional walls surrounding him wouldn't allow the kind of weakness to let someone that close, but Allison didn't understand why the thought made *her* feel even more vulnerable.

"Maybe not," she admitted as she grabbed her purse from her desk and ducked around him to reach the hallway, "but at least I can be there for my sister."

Something she'd failed to do for the past three years, and the weight of that remorse overrode her current feeling of guilt for slipping into the elevator and ignoring Zach as he called out after her.

Chapter Six

As Allison pulled into her sister's driveway, Bethany stepped out from the open garage, pushing her windblown hair back from her face. A dozen various sized boxes filled the driveway along with a miniature mattress that Allison bet still weighed a ton. Zach was right about one thing—she wouldn't be able to carry the furniture upstairs by herself. But with the pieces still in boxes and the mattress wrapped in protective plastic, she could at least drag everything into the garage.

A burst of wind practically tore the car door from her hand, and Allison hurried up the driveway. "It's going to be okay," she called out. "I've got a plan."

Surprisingly, her sister smiled. "I know."

"You do?"

Bethany nodded. "Your boss called a few minutes after I got off the phone with you."

It was the last thing Allison expected her sister to say. "Zach?"

Bethany waited until Allison hurried up the driveway and ducked into the garage and out of the wind. "He told me about the guy."

Rather than repeat yet another one of her sister's statements, Allison waited for Bethany to explain what "guy."

"He said Brad would be here in a half an hour and that he'd move everything inside and put the furniture together." She frowned. "Zach said you left in such a hurry that you forgot to give him the address here."

Why would Zach send someone to help? The unexpected kindness knocked the wind out of Allison's anger and left her drifting.

"Is something wrong?" Bethany asked.

"No, of course not." She certainly couldn't tell her sister she was mad at Zach and wanted to hold on to her anger because that emotion was easier, safer than the attraction she felt. And no way would she admit that *she* wanted to be the one to help, the one to come to the rescue. That would be far too petty and far too small.

"Be sure to thank Zach for this," Bethany said, big sister reminding little sis of her manners.

"Yeah, I will," Allison grumbled, not sounding the least bit thankful. And maybe she was that petty, that small after all.

Two hours later, gratitude edged petty and small aside. Brad, the guy Zach sent to help, was about six-five and weighed much as Allison, Bethany and the baby combined. It had taken some serious lifting to cart everything inside. From there, Brad went about breaking down the boxes and assembling the dresser, crib, changing table and rocking chair, thanks to a half a dozen tools Allison couldn't begin to name pulled from a box roughly the size of an overnight bag.

The furniture was huddled in the middle of the nursery

because they had yet to paint the walls the soft yellow Bethany wanted. The color would be a perfect contrast to the white furniture while the sheets, blankets and accessories she'd picked out were all in matching pastels.

The room was still a little bare, but at least now it was starting to look like a nursery. And Bethany seemed to be moving forward instead of staying stuck in separation limbo—like time would somehow fail to move on until she and Gage reconciled.

While Brad put the furniture together, Allison had helped Bethany move the rocking chair around the room, trying to find the perfect spot that would allow her a view out the window without being hit by the full afternoon sun. As Bethany rocked gently, her hand on her rounded stomach, a far-off look crossed her features.

"You'll be holding your baby in no time," Allison told her sister.

"I can't wait," Bethany said, but her smile was a little shaky, and Allison knew her sister had to be thinking about Gage.

"Seems like yesterday I was putting baby furniture together for my own kid," Brad said, his dark eyes twinkling as he gave the crib a shake. From what she could see, the sturdy piece didn't move an inch.

"We really appreciate you doing this, especially on such short notice."

"No problem. I told Zach if he ever needed a favor, all he had to do was call."

Sincerity shown in the man's eyes. From what Allison could tell, Brad seemed like a good guy. A beer-drinking, poker-playing, sports-on-the-weekend kind of guy. She already knew he drove a truck, and if his baseball hat could be believed, the occasional lawn tractor.

He was not, however, the kind of guy Allison would ever have figured to be friends with Zach Wilder.

Curiosity itched like poison oak, but she refused to scratch. It didn't matter why or how Brad and Zach came to be friends. She was grateful for their help—end of story.

"So, how do you know Zach?"

"Bethany!" Allison protested, her own vows falling to the wayside thanks to her sister's simple curiosity. "That's none of our business."

Her eyes wide, Bethany held out her hands in surrender. "Sorry. Didn't know it was a state secret!"

"I don't think it is," Brad chuckled. "We actually met through my wife. He stopped to do her a favor, and I've owed him ever since. I didn't really think I'd have the chance to pay him back, so I'm grateful you two ladies needed help."

Maybe she could look at it that way, Allison thought. As helping out Brad rather than accepting help from Zach....

Coward, the voice rejoined.

And, yeah, if Allison were honest with herself, that was more like it. She was afraid to see this side of Zach. Gorgeous or not, the cool-headed, cold-hearted businessman was someone Allison could resist. She didn't need someone like that in her life, *refused* to have someone like that in her life.

She'd already known it wouldn't be that easy, and that not even Zach could be so one-dimensional as she'd learned Friday night on a chandelier-lit dance floor. But the last thing she needed was anything that would make him even more attractive.

Once Brad left, amid multiple thanks from both women, Bethany ran her hand along the crib's closely spaced guardrails. "So," she said, her voice more matter-of-fact than curious, "are you going to tell me what's up with you and Zach?"

"Nothing's up. We're working together on a project."

"If there's nothing going on, how do you explain this?"

her sister challenged, waving a hand at the nearly completed nursery.

Explain this... Still at a loss, Allison wryly said, "Maybe he's decided he can't do without me at work, and he knows if I tried to put all this stuff together, I'd have to take off for a week."

"Not to mention the extra time for someone else to take it all apart and put it back together the right way," Bethany murmured, a slight smile tilting the corners of her mouth.

"Ouch," Allison protested, holding a hand to her wounded heart. "That hurts." But she wasn't the least bit offended by her sister's ribbing. It had been far too long since her sister had teased her.

And Allison supposed she had Zach to thank for that as well.

When she left Bethany's later that evening, Allison had every intention of heading home. The storm had washed the streets clean, leaving shallow pools that reflected the red, yellow and green of the stoplights and filled the air with the clean scent of rain. It was the perfect kind of evening to fix a cup of tea, curl up with a good book, turn the air conditioner down and pretend the weather was actually cold.

Besides, it was after seven o'clock. The workday had long since ended at Knox...for everyone but Zach. Allison didn't doubt for one minute he'd still be at his desk working. *And he'll be in first thing tomorrow morning,* she reminded herself. *So you can thank him then.* But despite the stern reminder, she took the turn that led down a very familiar road.

And not simply because she drove the street to work every day.

Allison pulled into the parking garage a few minutes later with a plan firmly in mind. She would thank Zach for his help, and that was it. She was climbing from the car when a familiar figure a few rows over caught her attention. She'd never admit it to anyone, didn't like admitting it to herself, but she'd recognize Zach's straight-shouldered, purposeful stride anywhere. He had a duffel bag slung over one shoulder. Judging by the intense frown on his face, he carried the weight of the world inside.

His car was parked on the other side of the garage, and he had yet to glance her way. She could slide back into the driver's seat and save her gratitude for the morning. No one needed to know she'd stopped by to see him...

Zach dropped the duffel bag inside the trunk and slammed it closed. But instead of circling the car and climbing inside the driver's seat, he stayed where he was, both hands braced against the trunk. Frustration rolled off him in waves, and Allison didn't have to ask how his work on the presentation had gone to know he wasn't happy.

And any thoughts of slipping away unnoticed fell by the wayside. She slammed the door harder than necessary to alert Zach to her presence before she strolled across the parking garage. "Hey, Zach."

Straightening, he turned to face her, whatever frustration she'd seen earlier wiped from his handsome face. If she didn't know better, she would have sworn nothing was wrong. If she didn't know *him* better...

Leaning a hip against the car, as if he didn't have a care in the world, Zach said, "What are you doing here? I thought you had a furniture emergency."

"I did, until you came to the rescue."

"I didn't do anything." Leaning forward slightly, he added, "I was working."

He was close enough to catch a hint of his aftershave, an intriguing combination of citrus and spice, and to see the flecks of ebony in his blue eyes. The combination sent an electric awareness streaking all the way down to her fingers and toes. Tempted to move closer, to sink her tingling fingers into his dark hair, Allison held her ground instead and did not give in to the urge to inhale even more of his scent. "You sent Brad. He was a huge help, and you were right. There was no way I could have moved all the furniture inside or put it together."

Expecting an I-told-you-so, Zach surprised her by merely shrugging. "I made a phone call. No big deal."

Except it was, even though Allison didn't want it to be. "I'll pay you back. Whatever Brad charges, give me the bill and I'll handle it."

Zach shook his head. "Forget it. The guy felt he owed me a favor."

"Why?"

He rolled his eyes at her demand. "You aren't gonna let this go, are you?"

"Nope. So you might as well tell me now and save me from asking another dozen times."

"His wife had a flat tire on the side of the road. It was late at night in a not-so-great part of town. I stopped and helped her out."

"And yet her husband seemed to think he owed you?"

"The spare seemed a little questionable, so I followed her home to make sure she didn't have any more problems. But really, it was—"

"No big deal. I got it."

"Anyway, I remembered that Brad worked for a moving company. It seemed like a good time to call in that favor."

A favor he never would have called in on his own, Allison knew. Which meant he'd done it for her.

Despite her supposed tenacity, Allison didn't ask him why, not even once. Instead, she said, "If you aren't going to let me pay you back for this, will you at least let me take you out to dinner?"

A look of surprise crossed his face, and Allison quickly worked to diffuse it. "Only as a thank-you."

She read the refusal in his eyes and told herself she was glad. Momentary rejection was a small price to pay for temporary insanity. Because, really, what was she thinking, asking Zach to dinner? Even as a simple show of gratitude, she had breached all kinds of barriers both of them knew better than to cross, and *thank goodness* he was going to say no—

"You're on."

"What?"

"Dinner. Where do you want to go?"

"Um…" Too stunned by his unexpected acceptance, Allison couldn't think of a single restaurant. "Are you sure you don't have other plans?"

"I was going to go to the gym." He frowned as if suddenly aware he'd altered his plans—not to mention broken his own rule—by saying yes.

Allison waited for him to change his mind, *wanted* him to change his mind, but then the image of Zach standing by the car, arms braced against the trunk flashed in her mind. And even though she knew she'd likely regret it later, she said, "You want to drive or should I?"

In the end, Zach drove as Allison figured he would. He asked her choice of restaurant, and she named a place close to work. She'd been to the Italian restaurant for lunch before and figured it was a safe pick. But she hadn't counted on the ambient switch from day to night. On the soft music playing in the background. On the low lighting or the soft glow of the centerpiece candles. And when the hostess led them to a secluded table in a far corner of the restaurant, Allison felt her face start to heat.

Would Zach see this as some kind of romantic come-on? The last thing she needed was for him to think she was hitting on him, especially when her invitation to dinner had been completely innocent, a thank-you for his help.

When Zach placed a hand at the small of her back, shivers ran up and down her spine—a silent mockery of her noble intentions—and Allison practically dropped into the chair. And, okay, so maybe her feelings weren't completely innocent, but she certainly had no intention of acting on those not-so-innocent feelings.

A smile kicked up the corners of his mouth as he murmured, "Nice place."

Jerking her gaze back up to his eyes, she hoped the way too romantic mood lighting at least hid the heat flooding her face. "I've only been here during the day. For lunch. When it's not so—"

"Not so what?" he prompted when her voice trailed off.

Romantic. Seductive. Intimate. The words bounced through her brain, along with the far more worrying thought that maybe it wasn't the restaurant. Maybe it was all Zach and she'd still feel the awareness humming beneath her skin even seated across from him in a fast food restaurant that boasted a jungle gym and red-haired clown.

"Not so crowded," Allison substituted, hoping mind reading wasn't one of Zach Wilder's considerable talents.

Judging by the knowing smile he gave, it just might be. Candlelight reflected in his eyes, the tiny dancing flames tempting her to come closer to the fire. "So, you were hoping for something a little more private?"

Allison forced a bland smile. "I was hoping for fast service. I have a very important presentation in the works, not to mention the Collins Jewelers groundbreaking tomorrow morning."

It was a cop-out, she knew, for *her* to bring up work, and it didn't even have the effect she'd counted on. She thought the mere mention of the presentation and groundbreaking ceremony would make Zach jump right back over the professional line they'd crossed, but instead he laughed, the flash of teeth and the spark in his eyes making him look very nonprofessional and even more appealing.

"How very conscientious of you, Ms. Warner. You might end up with a promotion after this."

Allison knew he meant the words as a compliment, but she had to suppress a shudder. That was the next to last thing she needed, second only to any kind of romantic involvement with Zach. She caught the speculative look in his expression but was saved from having to answer questions by the waitress's arrival. The woman placed two glasses of ice water in front of them along with a basket of warm, mouthwatering breadsticks. She ordered the cheese ravioli while Zach placed an order for a trio of lasagna, spaghetti and manicotti that honestly did sound like plenty of food for three people.

"You know, I realized something when I picked you up at your place the other night."

"Uh-oh. What deep dark secret of mine have you uncovered?"

"The thing is," Zach leaned closer, erasing the distance the table put between them, "I couldn't help noticing...you don't have an alarm system."

Allison jerked back, swallowing an abrupt laugh as well as healthy dose of embarrassment. Had she really thought Zach was coming on to her? Had she really expected him to say he'd noticed something attractive, remarkable, *irresistible* about her?

Idiot, she thought, giving in to the laughter. "Got to hand it to you, Zach. You are quite the salesman. I didn't even see that one coming."

Drawing back slightly, he blinked in surprise before protesting, "That wasn't a sales pitch. You're a single woman, living alone—"

Still convinced she was being sold, she waved a careless hand. "Yeah, yeah, I know, but I live in a good neighborhood."

"Good neighborhoods are usually the ones where homes are broken in to. Thieves don't bother to break in if you have nothing to steal. And the bad guys aren't always looking to rip off a flat screen TV."

Refusing to let him scare her, she protested, "Zach—"

"Look, just listen. When I was a teenager, it was my mom and me. After my dad died, I worked my way through high school, doing the usual jobs—fast food, car washes, waiter. Anything that had hours available evenings and weekends. Anyway, one night when I was still at work, my mom was home alone. She was getting ready for bed when she heard a sound from the back patio. My mother's a brave woman, not the kind to jump at shadows or call the police because she hears a noise. She figured it was the neighbor's cat or that the wind had knocked a flowerpot off a ledge. So, she went downstairs to check it out. She'd just reached the bottom step when she saw him."

Feeling like she was listening to an urban legend told around a flickering campfire—only this story was true— Allison swallowed. "Someone had broken in?"

"My mom didn't get a good look at the guy. She turned and ran back upstairs. She knew she'd be trapped there, but he was blocking the back door, and she would have had to run right in front of him to get to the front door. So she ran upstairs and locked the bedroom door. She told the guy she was calling the cops, but 911 had her on hold and this psycho was pounding on a hollow door with a push button lock that didn't have a chance of keeping him out until the cops showed up."

Allison didn't want to even imagine herself in that position, but it was impossible not to empathize. "She must have been terrified."

"She was, but luckily, I got off work early that night. I think the guy heard the car door slam and was too stupid or too stoned to realize there was no way the cops could have gotten to the house so fast. He split out the back before I even knew anything was wrong."

"And your mother was okay?"

"Yeah, she was fine, but we got an alarm system the next week." Zach took a drink of water before he added, "I struck up a conversation with George Hardaway, the guy who did the install, and a few months later, he hooked me up with a job at Knox."

"When you were still a teenager?" Allison knew Zach had worked at the company for at least five years, the watch he'd received told her that, but she hadn't realized he worked there so much longer.

"Yeah, it's going on a dozen years now. I started out installing on weekends and evenings when I was in high school and then in college. After I graduated I moved into customer service and then sales."

"No wonder you're so good at it. With a sales pitch like that, who could refuse?"

Zach frowned. "It's not a sales pitch."

Regret instantly swamped Allison. She'd meant her comment as a compliment, but she could see how he might have taken it as one of her flippant remarks. "Zach—"

"Here you go. Cheese ravioli and our signature trio." The waitress's arrival interrupted Allison's apology, and she had to wait until she'd told the young woman that no, she didn't need water, yes, she'd like grated parmesan on her ravioli, and no, thank you, she didn't need anything else before she could continue.

"I'm sorry, Zach. I didn't mean to trivialize what happened to your mother."

"It's okay."

Thinking his acceptance of her apology happened way too easily, Allison went on. "I only meant you have a personal experience your clients can relate to." One that was much more meaningful than the facts and figures he'd quoted Riana or the techno-speak he used when telling Daryl about the Collins presentation.

"Allison, it's okay. You don't have to apologize. It's just it's not a sales pitch," he repeated. "I've never told anyone that story, certainly not a client. I'm selling a product that I think is the best on the market. That's why people should buy it, not because I've figured out a way to exploit my own past. I wouldn't do that, wouldn't cross the line between my personal life and professional life that way."

Zach's eyebrows drew together, as if he couldn't figure out why he'd crossed that same line to tell *her* the story. He dropped his gaze to the plate in front of him and dug in like there'd be no food tomorrow, and Allison did the same.

But the question played through her thoughts for the rest of the evening.

This was not a date. Zach repeated the reminder as he drove Allison back to her car. He would drop her off, make sure her car started, wave goodbye, and tell her he'd see her in the morning.

At work.

This was not a date, so he had no reason to think about walking Allison to her car or kissing her good-night…even if he had spent far too much time gazing across the table at her, drawn by the way the candlelight made the blond highlights in her hair shimmer, the hint of gold in her green eyes, and the solitary dimple that flashed when she smiled.

She shifted, crossing her legs, and drawing his attention to the toned calves revealed by her knee-length skirt. Somehow, despite the fact that the passenger seat certainly hadn't *moved,* she seemed closer. The subtle scent of her perfume teased his senses, and when he reached for the gearshift, Allison's bare knee was mere inches away. He wouldn't even have to stretch to run his hand along her thigh.

Zach shifted into fourth gear with far more force than necessary, and the engine roared in response, giving voice to the sudden surge of testosterone in his body. He sensed Allison staring at him and muttered, "Sorry. Gears stuck."

He refused to glance her way as she offered a noncommittal sound that could have meant she bought the excuse or, just as easily, could have been her way of calling him a total liar. Mentally shaking his head at the unaccustomed display of nerves, Zach couldn't figure out what was wrong with him. He was acting like a kid out on his first date. Which was ridiculous since he was no kid.

And this *wasn't* a date!

Turning into the parking lot a few minutes later with a feeling of relief, Zach gazed at the Knox building. The backlit logo glowed against the glass and chrome wall, and if ever he had needed a sign to remind himself of his goals, it was now. Work came first. With the Collins presentation and the promotion on the horizon, a reminder shouldn't have been necessary. That he needed one, well that—that was all Allison's fault.

He drove into the parking garage and pulled into the spot beside her car. Drop her off, say good-night, and see her *at work* the next morning. That was all he needed to do to get back on an even keel and off the seesaw of unacceptable emotions. Ignoring the voice that warned it might not be so easy, Zach shifted to face Allison. He kept one wrist draped over the steering wheel and the engine running, sure signs that he wouldn't be getting out, wouldn't be walking the ten steps to see her to her car. All he had to do was say—

"Thanks again for your help with the furniture guy. I'll see you tomorrow morning!" Allison's bright and shiny farewell could have been stolen directly from the script he'd written in his mind, and she hopped out of the car before he could think twice about what had happened.

Unfortunately, he cut the engine and jumped out to follow her before he had time to think about what the hell he was doing. "Allison."

"Yeah?" she glanced back over her shoulder as if surprised he hadn't let her get away clean, and by now, his brain had caught up with his body and was reminding him this was a very *bad* idea.

But Zach couldn't help rounding the front of the car and walking over to her side. He reached down to open the car door she'd already unlocked by remote. The small key chain alarm reminded him of their earlier conversation, and he grasped hold of it like a lifeline, uncertain what else he might have said, might have *done*…

"Don't think I've forgotten about the security system."

"I know you haven't, and I've been seriously considering it. Not for myself—" she held up a hand in protest "—but for my sister. I don't like that she's all alone."

"You mean Bethany?"

"She's the only sister I have."

"But she's—" Zach cut himself off, realizing he was encroaching on some *highly* personal territory.

"She's what?"

"Pregnant," he blurted out.

"Yes, she is," Allison said with a sigh. "Her husband moved out a few months ago."

He hadn't asked, Zach consoled himself. Allison offered up the information. He wasn't breaking his rules, crossing any boundaries.

But as he'd already suspected, Allison wasn't a woman to put much stock in rules or boundaries, and the information kept spilling out. "They always seemed so happy, you know, the perfect couple."

A wistful note whispered alongside her words, a longing for what her sister had once had—a happy marriage, one-half of a perfect couple—and Zach's gut clenched.

"It was such a shock when they separated, especially since it was right after Bethany got pregnant. And she's been so closemouthed about the whole thing. She won't even tell me what happened."

Allison swung her hands out from her side, an empty, frustrated gesture. He would have thought the sisters the type to share *everything,* so no wonder Bethany's silence bothered Allison.

She's lonely, he realized suddenly. For all her ties to her family, Allison was lonely. If only she'd apply herself to her career, she could—

Work sixty hours a week, spend as little time at home as possible so she wouldn't notice how empty it is, how quiet... the way you do?

The thought hit out of nowhere, a blow he hadn't seen coming, and he couldn't find the momentum to fight it off. He didn't know what stunned him more, the idea that he was lonely or that he and Allison had something in common.

"I'm sure things will work out." The meaningless platitude was the best he could offer, but even in the parking lot's dim light, he saw the disappointment in Allison's eyes, as if she'd been hoping for something more.

She would soon figure out when it came to personal insight, he was *not* the man for the job.

"Right," she said with a forced smile. "Hopefully, Bethany and Gage will get back together before the baby's born."

Zach's hand tightened on the edge of the door. "Yeah, well, it might be best if he *doesn't* come back."

A frown wrinkling her forehead, Allison stared up at him. "How can you say that?"

"Look, if the guy's not committed to his family, they're better off without him. Otherwise, that kid's gonna grow up hearing nothing but how he's a burden, an anchor holding his dad back from the success he could have had. No way is that kind of a childhood best for the kid."

Allison studied him closely. "Is that what happened to you, Zach? Is that how your dad made you feel?"

Realizing the load of emotional garbage he'd dumped at her feet, he took a step back as if a few inches of space might shield him from the awareness—the *pity*—in her green gaze. Inches wouldn't do. *Light-years* wouldn't be enough, Zach thought. He didn't know why he kept telling her secrets he never shared; why he kept crossing lines he never crossed...

"Zach, wait!" Allison's heels struck the concrete seconds before her hand closed around his arm.

At the touch of her hand, Zach felt his control snap. Like some tiny thread was all that held him in check instead of a lifetime of lessons and rules. But once it was gone, it was gone and there was no holding back.

Standing in the soft glow from the security lights, her hair gleaming like gold, her eyes wide with concern, Zach didn't know what was worse, the compassion he read in her expression or the sudden desire he knew was written in his.

All he knew was that if he was going to break the rules, they might as well be ones worth breaking. Sliding his hand beneath her hair, he caught the nape of her neck and pulled her into a kiss.

Allison had known she'd pushed Zach too far, forced him to reveal something so personal about his childhood. Those brief sentences about his father had given away more than he wanted her to know, his own admissions catching him off guard and knocking him out of balance. She'd expected him to give her the silent treatment, remind her that nothing mattered but work, or possibly even ask for a replacement to help with the Collins proposal.

She never expected the kiss. As startled as she was, there was still a moment when Zach's gaze met hers. A split second when she could have turned aside or pulled away. And he would have let her go. Allison knew it as fact, as undeniable as the inky darkness of his hair or the startling blue of his eyes. But she didn't turn aside or pull away. And as his mouth claimed hers, she didn't care that the kiss was about Zach regaining control of the situation and taking back whatever ground he thought he'd lost in letting her see that heartbreaking glimpse into his childhood.

Because when he kissed her, there was nothing controlled about it and there was nothing he could take that Allison wouldn't freely give...

She clung to his shoulders as she lost herself in his kiss. Each pass of his lips over hers stoked an answering desire inside Allison. She parted her lips, welcoming his tongue, the intimate contact fueling the flames as she caught a hint of the chocolate mints they'd shared before leaving the restaurant. The combination had always been one of her favorites, but now, with the added taste of Zach's kiss, Allison knew she'd never enjoy them the same way again. Because she'd likely never enjoy them *this* way again.

Her conscience tried to butt in and remind her where they were, *who* they were, but Allison blocked the voice out, teasing Zach's tongue with her own until his husky groan was all she heard. His hands slid from her shoulders and down her back, his fingers pressing into her hips and pulling her closer. Her breasts met his chest and the strength of his thigh pressed between hers, but the contact was nowhere near enough. Too many clothes, too many barriers. But her body didn't care;

her heart pounded wildly and threatened to jump from her chest, desperate to join with his.

When he lifted his head, she fought back a disappointed moan and reluctantly opened her eyes. At first, Zach's face filled her vision, her senses, her world. She blinked. Once. Twice. Each time, her focus widened, and she gradually became aware of her surroundings.

The Knox parking garage—again.

One of these days, we've got to get a room.

Zach jerked back so abruptly, for a moment Allison feared she'd said the words out loud. She was pretty sure she hadn't voiced the thought; just as well since she could already see it wasn't one Zach shared. At least not once he stopped feeling and started thinking.

"Allison—"

"Don't," she said, interrupting whatever "business first" speech he planned to give. Her breathing was still ragged, her pulse still pounded, and even filled with regret, the deep murmur of his voice almost sent her back into his arms. But already the shields were coming down, the walls going up, as the businessman persona hid the real man she was only starting to get to know. And that loss left Allison feeling so much more bereft than his physical withdrawal had.

She crossed her arms over her stomach as if that futile action might keep the emptiness at bay. "I already know everything you're going to say."

Zach stared at her before running a frustrated hand through his hair and muttering, "I'm glad one of us does."

The knowledge that the kiss affected him as much as it had her didn't help Allison's skin to cool any, but she pushed forward anyway. "We work together, and you don't mix business and pleasure. Even if you did, business always comes first. You have too much at stake with the Collins proposal to take your eye off the ball for even a second, so you certainly don't have time to start something with me."

The words were Zach's, but the fire behind them definitely belonged to Allison, even though she'd tried her best to smother it and deliver the words with the same cool indifference he'd once used. Tried...and failed miserably.

"You're right," he said, agreeing to her disappointment with everything she said, but then he stepped closer, close enough for her to see the still-burning desire his distance and her words hadn't extinguished, "and yet you couldn't be more wrong."

Chapter Seven

The next morning brought a perfect spring day with clear blue skies overhead. Not a single cloud marred the Collins Jewelers groundbreaking. The slightly muddy patch of dirt didn't look like much now, but poster boards showed drawings of what the impressive slate and glass fronted building would look like.

"Thank you all for coming today," James Collins said as he posed for cameras in a gray designer suit with an official shovel and hard hat that were only for show. "This is an exciting moment and a new chapter for Collins Jewelers."

Leaning close, Zach murmured, "Looks like Knox is the only security company here."

The warmth of his breath chased goose bumps across Allison's skin. The words were strictly business, like everything else they'd talked about since last night's kiss, but her body didn't care. They might have stopped short of intimate touches and arousing caresses, but like a movie scene on pause, she felt caught in that moment, in the promise of *more, more,*

more... All it would take was a single touch, and she'd be right back in the fevered pitch where Zach had left her twice now. How many times did the red-hot promise of a look, a touch, a kiss have to turn into ice-cold business before she stopped allowing Zach to push her buttons?

It wasn't fair, she thought, stealing glances at him from the corner of her eye. The morning sun gleamed in his dark hair. A cool breeze molded his white dress shirt to his chest and abs while flipping his tie this way and that like a woman's playful fingers. He had his hands in his pockets, pulling the black trousers tight against his thighs.

If he wasn't so gorgeous—but that wasn't the problem. At least, not entirely. She'd worked around enough good-looking men since coming home to know more than simple proximity to a hot guy was at work here.

Work. Here. Trying to focus on Zach's words instead of the havoc he'd created inside her, Allison murmured, "That's a good sign."

The morning had gone off without a hitch, but she was still suspicious of Riana Collins's invitation. The other woman wanted Allison at this ceremony, and she doubted she'd appreciate the reasons why. So far, Riana was simply enjoying the spotlight at her father's side, but Allison doubted the gold cuff and diamond watch were all she had up her black cashmere sleeves.

As James took a moment to acknowledge the longtime employees he'd brought from other stores to head up this new venture, Zach reached into his pocket for his phone. He glanced at the screen before looking over at James who was still surrounded by media and his own employees. Still, Allison was a little surprised when he didn't tuck the phone away and let the call go to voice mail.

She was even more surprised when she heard the warmth in his voice. "Hey, Sylvie. How are you?" He barely got out the greeting before a burst of sound came from the other end of the line. Allison couldn't hear the words, but she picked up on the urgency in the tone and read the worried frown on Zach's handsome face.

"I'll take care of it. Don't worry." His reassurances must have worked—and why not? The low murmur of his voice could have talked Allison's weakening resistance into almost anything. He listened for another moment before laughing. "I'm going to hold you to that, Syl."

After saying goodbye, Zach immediately began dialing. He spoke with customer service, making it clear he expected a tech to show up at Sylvie's within the hour. Pocketing the phone, he said, "Sorry about that."

"Important client?" Allison asked casually even as she imagined another woman like Riana—bold, beautiful and connected—who had him on speed dial.

Zach shot her an amused look, telling Allison her question might have been a little too obvious. "Sylvie is an eighty-year-old grandmother who lives in Sun City. She was one of my first sales at Knox, way before I moved into corporate sales. Her family wanted her to have the alarm for their own peace of mind, but the technology is a little beyond her. She's had some electrical work done and turning off the power has reset the system to the default setting. She needs help getting her own preferences reprogrammed."

"So she called you?"

Six years after he made the sale.

"It's no big deal," he insisted gruffly, but it *was* a big deal to Allison.

Who would have thought he'd still take an interest in a client so many years later? Or that he'd be so endearingly embarrassed by it? He'd done the same thing last night, hiding his efforts to help rather than broadcasting them the way most guys would. "I'm sure Sylvie's family thinks it is."

"First rule in business. Keep the client happy."

And that was easy. Cut-and-dried. Black and white. But keeping *people* happy, making his father proud—that had been impossible.

"Oh, Zach." Allison heard the tenderness and warmth in the soft murmur of his name, but she couldn't help it. Sunlight was seeping through the cracks in her defenses, softening her heart like chocolate left on the windowsill.

"Okay, stop." He pinned her with a look that should have instantly turned her heart back into a rock-solid, frostbitten lump but didn't. Behind the abrupt command, Allison could see Zach building his own defenses back up as quickly as hers were coming down. "Don't make me out to be something I'm not."

"I'm not. I won't," she promised, but only because she didn't have to. She wanted Zach exactly as he was—flaws and all—even though she knew how dangerous that wanting could be. How open and vulnerable it would leave her...

The feeling only increased as Riana edged Allison out of the way to place a proprietary hand on Zach's arm and offer her a self-satisfied smile. "There are some people I'd like Zach to meet. You'll excuse us, won't you, Allison?"

I know what Zach wants and better yet, we both know I can give it to him.

Allison watched silently as Zach shook hands with the mayor. The words Riana had spoken at the benefit were far more than a meaningless boast. Riana Collins could give Zach what he wanted. An in with her father. Business contacts with some of the most important people in the state.

And Zach was in his element—confident, charismatic and in control. Little wonder Riana wanted to claim him for herself.

Allison felt the same. But not because Zach was ambitious or successful or going places. Instead, she was falling for the man Zach could be despite all those things. The guy who'd helped her sister, the salesman who went out of his way to reassure a little old lady in Sun City, the son who spoke of his mother with pride in his voice. *That* was the Zach Wilder who could make her forget Kevin, who could slip past her defenses and make her want...

But would that matter if in the end, Zach wanted more? More than she could offer, more than she could give? She'd loved Kevin, but that certainly hadn't been enough to keep him from resenting her success or taking her work and passing it off as his own. Zach was ten times more driven and dedicated than her ex ever dreamed of being. Wouldn't that make Zach so much harder to please?

"I don't blame you, you know."

Lost in thoughts of whether Zach would even give romance a chance, Allison started at the sound of Riana's pseudo-sympathetic voice. "Blame me for what?"

"For trying to hold on to Zach. He's smart, gorgeous, successful." Riana scraped Allison from head to toe with a look suggesting she was clutching onto Zach's coattails by her fingernails. "But sooner or later, he's going to realize you're only holding him back."

As much as Allison hated to admit it, Riana had a point. The key to any relationship with Zach would be knowing that in the end, she'd have to let him go.

"I'm looking forward to our meeting next week," Zach told James Collins. He'd counted on a chance to talk to the other man after the failure of his last two attempts, but his gaze kept wandering back to Allison.

He'd seen something in her eyes earlier, something soft and dangerous. She'd acted like he was some kind of hero when he was only doing his job. And okay, so maybe Sylvie wasn't his typical client, but he hadn't totally gone out of his way to help her. Not really. Not like Allison made it seem.

She hid it well, but a slight frown pulled at her eyebrows, her expressive green eyes troubled by whatever subtle, or not so subtle, dig Riana made, and Zach caught himself leaning in that direction. Ready to rush to Allison's aid even though he didn't know what he was so worried about. The night of the benefit, hadn't Allison already proved she could hold her own with Riana Collins? More importantly, he *trusted* her to hold her own.

Make Collins feel like Knox is the right choice.

He still didn't think he needed to wrap the presentation in hearts and flowers, but if he trusted Allison to handle Riana, maybe he should consider what she'd suggested.

As James Collins moved on to take a photo with the lead architect, Zach had his chance to ingratiate himself in with the mayor and councilmen Riana had introduced him to. But as with all dealings with Riana, serious strings were attached. If he didn't dance to her tune like the marionette she wanted, she'd cut ties in an instant. He preferred to make his own contacts like he always had.

After saying his farewells, Zach walked back over to Allison. She was dressed for the outdoor meeting in a button-down camel-colored shirt, a denim skirt and calf length boots. Her hair shimmered in the sunlight, catching the warm rays, and Zach fisted his hands in his pockets, denying the urge to bury his fingers in the honeyed strands. She'd used some kind of shiny lip gloss that reminded him of the strawberry they'd shared the night of the benefit. He hadn't been able to get the scent or the flavor or *Allison* out of his mind since.

"You okay?" he asked, keeping his voice low to avoid being overheard.

"Why wouldn't I be?" The slightly facetious tone told

Zach Riana had struck a nerve, but Allison wasn't going to fill him in.

"I guess it was that whole method acting thing. I wanted to make sure my pretend girlfriend isn't the jealous type."

Allison gave a sound of disbelief. "Jealous, ha! I trust my pretend boyfriend completely. We have a strong pretend relationship. One built on honesty and respect."

Even though she hadn't lost her teasing smile, and Zach hadn't stopped staring at the dimple it revealed, he caught a hint of longing underscoring her words, reminding him of what little she'd told him of her ex. Kevin, with the wandering eyes and wandering hands. "That's what you deserve, Allie."

And *that* was what he would have told Allison last night in the parking garage if she'd let him. Even though every excuse she'd given for him to pull away had been logical and valid and, hell, nothing he hadn't said before, the real reason was because he couldn't be the kind of man she wanted. And he didn't want either of them thinking otherwise.

"But I'm not—"

She stopped his words with a touch, a hand on his arm in a move too casual to raise eyebrows in a business setting, but the warmth of her skin against his felt far more intimate than it should. "It's all pretend, remember?"

An adult version of a childlike game where no one got hurt because everyone knew it wasn't real. But Allison wasn't saying—she didn't mean—she couldn't be suggesting they play the game for something other than Riana's benefit... Could she?

Zach was spared from coming up with an answer he didn't have when a voice called his name.

"Zach Wilder?"

He turned at the sound of the deep baritone, but not in time to avoid a blow between the shoulder blades that nearly knocked the breath from his lungs. He looked up to meet the dark gaze of a man who towered over him by nearly a foot and outweighed him by one-hundred pounds. "You probably don't remember me, but you—hell, you look just like your old man."

The slap on the back was nothing compared to the right hook those words delivered. *Just like your old man.*

Oblivious to the hit Zach had taken, the other man went on. "Me and Nathan, man, we went to high school together. I'm Ted Thompson."

The name flashed across the screen in Zach's mind— grainy footage from football games taped decades ago. "You were the center."

"Yeah!" The recognition earned Zach a clap on the shoulder. "Me and your dad, we had the greatest time in high school. He ever tell you about that?"

Nathan Wilder had talked of little else. His high school glory days were all he'd had. That and the million dollar dreams his wife and child had cost him.

"We lost touch after graduation. Don't know if you remember, but I went on to college and pro ball. Blew my knee out after five years in the NFL, but not before I got this." Ted held out a huge hand sporting an equally enormous ring—the kind awarded to Super Bowl winners. "So what's Nate been up to?"

Zach was vaguely aware of Allison sliding her palm down his arm to take his hand. The squeeze she gave caused pinpricks along his skin, as if his entire body had somehow gone numb and was now beginning the painful sensation of waking up. "I'm sorry, Mr. Thompson," she said, "but Zach's father passed away over ten years ago."

The big man swore beneath his breath. "I'm sorry. I didn't hear. I'd always hoped we'd get the old gang back together, toss the pigskin around and talk about the old days. Your dad—" Ted shook his head. "I always thought he could have been great."

It was the story of Nathan Wilder's life—what could have been. Zach knew it all too well, but his life would have a different ending. He would succeed where his father had failed. Nothing, and no one, would stand in his way.

As Zach drove Allison back to Knox, he could feel the weight of her gaze on him, her green eyes filled with a sympathy he didn't deserve. Her voice was soft when she told him, "I lost my dad six months ago." Reaching out, she covered the hand he'd fisted on his thigh, her soothing touch adding to his sense of guilt. "It was the hardest thing I've ever gone through. I still have days when I can't believe he's gone. I have so many things to tell him, so many things I wished I'd said…"

"Don't," he bit out, his voice sharper than he'd intended. He could have simply nodded, silently accepting that they had a shared sense of grief. But he couldn't do it. Couldn't cheapen Allison's genuine sorrow by pretending to feel something he didn't anymore than he could find the will to pull his hand away from hers.

"It's not the same, Allie." He waited until he reached a red light to meet her gaze and tell her, "My relationship with my father wasn't anything like you had with yours."

He was quiet for a minute. "My dad was the quarterback of his high school football team. His team only lost one game that he started, and he took them to the state championship three years in a row. He was the golden boy."

Zach never knew that man. The unwanted responsibility and burden of marriage and fatherhood had quickly tarnished that shine. "He was looking forward to a college scholarship. He never missed going to the Fiesta Bowl and thought he'd play in a couple of bowl games before moving on to the pros."

"Those are some big dreams," Allison agreed with enough feeling to tell him she knew the story didn't have a happy ending.

"My father's senior year, he got my mother pregnant. They both graduated high school, but my dad didn't go on to college. He started working in the warehouse of a shipping company. He *hated* that job. No cameras or cheerleaders when you spend your life standing at a conveyor belt. My dad's dreams ended with a walk down the aisle, and he never stopped resenting me and my mom for ruining the life he could have had. It's like Ted said back there. My dad was the ultimate could-have-been."

"You know, it doesn't have to be that way. Having a family has its own rewards. And it's not without cameras or cheerleaders. People who love you and celebrate all the moments and milestones in life."

It sounded good. Too good. Kind of like that game of pretend. But fourteen years of real life had taught Zach a harsher, darker lesson of what *family* could mean.

"My father would disagree."

Allison sighed as she pulled her hand away. And even though it was for the best, he felt the loss of her touch immediately. The selfishness of that need was too much of a reminder of Nathan Wilder, a man who only cared about his wants, his desire, his lost dreams, to hell with his wife and child.

"Did you ever stop to think your father was wrong?" she asked. "Wrong about family? Wrong about you?"

"Even if he was, even if you're right about how great family can be, that doesn't change who I am and what I want."

"The Collins account."

"That's right," Zach agreed, feeling defensive even though Allison hadn't argued, hadn't tried to convince him maybe he could be a family man *and* a businessman, too.

"Wouldn't it be nice, though, just once to have someone to share in that success?"

He'd never been interested in sharing. His accomplishments were his…and his alone. But for the first time in his life, Zach was struck by how hollow that victory sounded.

After a morning filled with meetings, it was almost noon when Zach stepped into his office and stopped short. He still wasn't used to seeing Allison there. With only a week left until the Collins presentation, he wouldn't have time to get used to seeing her. But that didn't stop him from taking a moment to watch her, unnoticed from just inside the doorway.

He had a perfect view of her profile as she sat at her desk, gazing at the computer screen—the elegant arch of her eyebrow, the high curve of her cheekbone, the delicate shape of her lips…

Working as much as he did, Zach didn't have the string of lovers or one-night stands some men liked to boast about. But he'd been with enough women for one kiss to blur into the next without any moment standing out as particularly memorable or earth-shattering. Until Allison.

Monday night's kiss had haunted him just like the one from the week before. Seductive and potent, it followed him home, slipping into his thoughts, sliding into his dreams, convincing his subconscious Allison was *there*. He'd reached out to pull her naked body down to his only to wake up alone…and wanting.

With any other woman, he might have suggested a fling—a red-hot affair to burn the sexual tension out of their systems. Hell, he'd even considered it after that first kiss before he found out they'd be working together. Before he got to know Allison. Despite the temp jobs she flitted to, one after another, she wasn't the kind of woman who treated relationships the same way. As much as she tried to hide it, hurt lingered in the shadows of her eyes whenever she spoke about her ex-boyfriend. She'd loved Kevin enough for their breakup to have left her heartbroken and vulnerable. The trendy clothes, the bright colors, and even her cocky attitude were all a façade to protect the real woman inside. A woman not nearly as tough as she pretended.

And even if she had been, Zach sensed getting over Allison wouldn't be so easy. That making love to her wouldn't be the end of his wanting, but the beginning…

Shaking off the discomforting thought, Zach cleared his throat as he crossed the room. "Daryl asked for an update on the Collins presentation, and I told him you've been…shopping?" He spoke the last word in a question, but he could clearly see the website she was surfing and a gold link bracelet with a heart charm on the screen.

"Yeah, right," she scoffed, but a hint of color came to her cheeks as if he had caught her doing something she shouldn't. "You have a seriously overinflated idea of what a temp receptionist pulls in. No way could I afford one of James Collins's pieces. But I thought about personalizing our—I mean, *your* presentation by importing pictures of his jewelry. Crediting the website, of course," she said as she clicked open a file showing how she'd incorporated both companies' logos as well as photos of some truly impressive pieces of jewelry.

"Wow, that's—you've done a great job."

Meeting with Daryl that morning, Zach hadn't had any idea how he was going to incorporate the *personal twist* his boss expected him to add to the Collins presentation, but after the groundbreaking yesterday, he'd made up his mind to see what Allison could do. He leaned closer to get a better look, but his focus was further challenged by the strawberry scent of her shampoo and the golden hair tucked behind the curve of her ear. He'd rested a hand against the back of her chair, his fingers within reach of her shoulder covered by a beige blouse embroidered with roses along a neckline that highlighted her delicate collarbones and gold locket resting between her breasts.

"We can do the same with the PowerPoint presentation. Something like this." She opened another program and clicked the mouse. Pictures of Collins's jewelry on a black background faded in and out between his slides. "We could also put a watermark behind the slides—either more of Collins's jewelry or maybe their logo. It would be subtle, so it wouldn't take away from the information you're presenting, but still leave a clear impression."

"I like that, but what about using our logo instead?" Zach suggested, warming to the idea.

"You're right. That's even better. It would show how Knox Security would be part of their stores, but always in the background, leaving the real focus on the jewelry." Allison clicked a few more times on the mouse, switching from his gradient shades of blue to gray to an image of Knox's logo. "How's that?"

"Perfect."

"Yeah?" She turned to him with a pleased grin that slowly faded as she realized how close he was.

Memories from their last kiss still hovered between them, dynamite waiting for another spark. It wouldn't take much, Zach thought as his gaze lowered to Allison's mouth, mere inches from his own. All he had to do was lean forward, just a little—

"Hi—oh, goodness, I hope I'm not interrupting."

Zach pulled back, and Allison practically sprang to her feet at the sound of the feminine voice. He took a deep breath, trying to regain total control before he turned, already knowing what he'd find.

His mother stood in the doorway, a bright smile on her face, looking as stylish as ever in a pair of gray wool slacks and lavender sweater. With her sleek, brunette pageboy and trim figure, Caroline Wilder was still a lovely woman who didn't look old enough to be his mother.

"Zach, sweetie." She sailed into the office and met him with a vanilla-scented kiss. The standard greeting failed to take him by surprise, but his jaw about hit the floor when Caroline circled the desk to embrace an equally stunned Allison. "And Allison, dear. It's so good to meet you. You'll have to forgive my ill-mannered son for not introducing us sooner."

"I, um—nice to meet you, too?"

Zach heard the question in her voice but had no explanation for his mother's out-of-character reaction. "I got a phone call from Danielle Jones yesterday. You remember her, don't you, Zach?"

The name rang a bell—a good friend of his mother's... and a breast cancer survivor. Realization hit his stomach and sank slowly to his gut.

"She was at the benefit last Friday and saw you together. She said the two of you were very circumspect but, well, Danielle's been happily married for twenty-five years. She knows people in love when she sees them. Danielle called me to get all the details, and I was forced to admit my own son tells me nothing about his personal life."

Because there'd never been anything to tell. There *still* was nothing to tell no matter what Danielle *thought* she saw. A couple in love? *Hardly.* But the six degrees of separation between his mother, Danielle Jones, and someone at the benefit who might report back to Riana Collins was way too close for Zach to tell the truth.

Meeting Allison's gaze, he caught the subtle shake of her head, the slight flare of panic in her widening green eyes as he walked over and pulled her to his side. He felt the slight flutter of reaction, a shiver that raced from her body to his as he slid an arm around her waist, the telltale sign of attraction making it hard for him to remember this was all for show.

"Mom." Zach cleared his throat. "This is Allison Warner. My girlfriend."

When Allison was a kid, she and her family had made the drive up to Flagstaff for a day in the snow more times than she could recall, but one trip always stayed fresh in her memory. Bethany had happily stacked snowmen together and flapped angel wings in the freshly fallen powder, but Allison was more adventurous. She'd wandered away from her family and found a hill perfect for sledding. Anticipating a fun ride, she'd pushed off and held on. But the hill was steeper than she thought, the ride scarier as she picked up more and more speed, knowing the only way she was going to stop was when she crashed.

Hard.

As she sat across the table from an ecstatic Caroline Wilder, Allison had that same sickening feeling now. The lie she and Zach started had taken off under its own power, gaining momentum until there was no stopping it. And Allison didn't know when or how it would happen, but she sensed another painful crash in her future.

"So, Allison, since my closedmouth son hasn't filled me in, tell me about yourself."

"Well, I was born and raised in Phoenix. I have an older sister, Bethany, and I'm about to become an aunt."

"Oh, how wonderful. Children are such a blessing," Caroline said, her smile at Zach clearly stating how much she loved her own child.

After hearing Zach talk about his childhood, meeting his mother took Allison by surprise. She hadn't expected the older woman to be so warm and loving. But not even the power of a mother's love could protect a child from his father's resentment. "I agree, Caroline. You must be so proud of Zach."

"Oh, I'm very proud of Zach's career. He's very driven to succeed. My fault, I'm afraid. I always pushed him to do his best. I saw it as encouragement, but I think I went too far, and I worry about him," Caroline confessed. "His personal life has always been lacking. Or at least it has been until now."

"I *am* still here, you know," Zach chimed in wryly.

"Oh, yes, the conversation would be much more interesting if you weren't." Caroline's eyes gleamed as she looked from Zach to Allison and back again. "So tell me how you met?"

Allison swallowed. Fooling Riana Collins was one thing. Lying to Zach's mother was so much worse. "We, um, met at Knox."

"It was Allison's first day," Zach supplied when her answer fell short on details. Reaching over, he caught her hand, his fingers lacing through hers in a way that felt so much more intimate than it should have. "She cut right in front of my car with a smile and a wave, and I knew I had to meet her. I ran to catch up with her in the elevator, and when our hands touched as we reached for the same button, I just…knew."

Staring into his blue eyes, the dark lashes and faint lines becoming so familiar, Allison's heart started to pound. She remembered that first day, that first look, that first touch exactly as he described, illuminated by a romantic, diffused light. But like a double-exposed photo, that image didn't completely whitewash a different version of those events. A far more likely version—Zach speeding through the parking garage, too focused on work to notice her in the crosswalk until the last minute, Zach running to catch the elevator on his way to a meeting.

But it was Zach's scenario working its way beneath her skin, making her pulse pound, and her knees weak. The deep murmur of his voice and the seductive promise in his eyes made her long to simply hang on and enjoy the ride while it lasted.

"So, Zach…" His mother's voice trailed off expectantly as she waited, most likely, for him to spill his heart out.

Allison had excused herself to go to the ladies' room, and other than strapping her to her chair, he'd had to let her go. Not that he blamed her. He could have used some time himself.

Something about telling the story of how they met felt… real. Like that first meeting, that initial moment of connection truly had been the start of something. But they couldn't both bolt from the table, so now he was stuck with his inquisitor of a mother, ready to drag all the details she could out of him.

Staring at the menu as if the decision between a grilled chicken sandwich or fresh fish was all-consuming, Zach debated his options. Even at lunch, the popular restaurant with its gleaming hardwoods and brass accents was loud enough he could pretend he hadn't heard her. Or he could feign ignorance and act like he didn't know what his mother was waiting for.

Glancing around for the waiter, he mumbled, "I wonder what the catch of the day is?"

"Hmm, my guess is salmon," Caroline said with a knowing lift to her eyebrows.

Zach couldn't help but laugh and shake his head. "I have never been able to pull anything over on you."

Growing up, he'd never been the type to get in trouble. After his father died, he'd been too busy working and helping out around the house to find time for the usual teenage pitfalls. Even so, his mother had always known at a glance if he'd had a bad day or if he was holding something back.

"And yet you still try," his mother remarked dryly. "But

why didn't you tell me about Allison before I had to hear about it from a third party?"

"Allison's...Allison," he said, trying to buy some time. If it came down to actually voicing a description, he'd need more than a few minutes. Judging by the time she spent consuming his thoughts, he could wax poetic about her wide green eyes, curved lips, flirtatious dimple and sassy, sexy attitude for hours. And wouldn't Caroline love *that*...

Deciding to stick with the easiest explanation, he said, "I noticed her that first day, but it was only when Daryl had the idea for the two of us to work together that we grew...closer. She has a great eye for detail, a way of seeing things I've missed."

"And?"

His mother's pale blue eyes saw way too much, and Zach longed to dive back into the menu. "She's doing a good job."

That was a gross understatement, and he knew it. Allison was smart and savvy. The work she'd done on the PowerPoint was sophisticated, stylish, and, yeah, he had to admit, sexy.

Words he'd use to describe Allison...

Whether his fingers were gripping a pen or tapping away at his computer, he could still feel the softness of her skin, the silk of her hair. He'd been downing coffee until caffeine practically buzzed along his nerve endings, but not even the hottest liquid could scald the taste of her from his tongue. All that when she *wasn't* around. When she was...

How many times had he caught himself watching her as she talked and imagining the movements of her lips against his own? How many times had he zeroed in on the sound of her laughter just to see the flash of that tempting dimple in her right cheek? And when she came close enough to touch, reaching for the phone or to take a closer look at his computer screen, it was all he could do not to pull her into his arms, to feel the curves and angles of her body pressed against him again…

His chair's armrests had permanent indention marks from gripping the padded leather as he tried to keep his desire under control.

"All very interesting, but not quite what I had in mind." His mother's voice broke into his thoughts, the matchmaker's gleam in her eyes more than obvious. "I want to know more about *you* and Allison. Is it serious between you two?"

Instant denial fired through his brain—he didn't do relationships; he wouldn't. But the words froze before they reached his throat, lodging there with a pressure that threatened to choke him. And not just because he wanted to keep the charade in place but because the words were a lie. The kiss they'd shared told him how *involved* he already was with Allison.

He couldn't explain that kiss anymore than he could his reasons for spilling his past. All he knew was that seeing Allison gaze up at him with a mixture of understanding and sympathy reflected in her gaze, he'd completely lost control of the conversation, of his emotions, of the high wire balancing act required to keep his relationship with Allison steady.

Why he thought kissing her would help him regain that control, he had *no* idea.

Just like he wasn't sure where the romanticized retelling of their first meeting came from. It was so unlike him, so out of character, he half expected his mother to call him on it. But Caroline's normally shrewd gaze was clouded by hope and happiness, and he'd better start laying the ground work for an ending to whatever love affair his mother was picturing him and Allison having or it would only make matters worse.

"Allison is an amazing woman. Any man would be lucky to have her by his side for the rest of his life," Zach said, realizing the words were one hundred percent true. "But I can't be that man."

"Zach—"

"You know me, Mom. You know me better than that," he said, almost desperate for Caroline to agree.

He felt like he'd reached a fork in the road. On the right was the paved, much-traveled path to business success. On the left, the rocky, dangerous terrain of personal territory. He knew what lay in that direction. Failure, misery, heartache. He could practically see his father's footsteps in the barren, desolate ground.

She sighed, the disappointment in her eyes hard to take, but Zach knew it could be so much worse. "A mother always dreams."

His childhood had taught him he couldn't trust dreams any more than he could trust love. Reality intruded, slicing through like the morning sun through a part in the curtains. Dreams rarely held up under the harsh light of day, and when they didn't come true, they turned into bitter reminders of what could have been.

"Your mom's really great," Allison said to Zach once they were back at the office.

"Yeah, she is. She really kept things together for us when I was younger. She'd held a couple of part-time jobs while my dad was alive, but once he died—it was just the two of us then, and those first few years were...rough. My mom didn't have much of a work history and only a high school diploma, but she got a job as a clerk in a department store and worked her way up to manager."

Fierce pride shone from his eyes, tugging at something inside Allison as she imagined Zach as a serious, solemn-eyed boy who learned early on that hard work equaled survival. That things like having fun and hanging out with friends didn't put food on the table, and her heart ached—for the boy he'd been and the man he was now. Was it any wonder Zach wouldn't ease up? Wouldn't let himself relax? Those childhood lessons had taught him everything could be taken away without warning.

The more she got to know Zach, the more she understood why he focused his heart and soul on his career. At Knox, he had everything his father had denied him—attention, recognition, and early on, Allison had spotted the fatherly affection Daryl Evans had for Zach—even if Zach did resent his interference just the way a real son would.

"My mom taught me to work hard but now..." Zach shook his head ruefully. "She's been on my case lately to relax, to take more time for myself."

"All of which makes me feel that much worse."

"Why?"

"Because she thinks we're really dating," Allison said, her voice barely above a whisper as if Caroline might somehow overhear. "Why did you let her think that?"

"We've come this far, and I can't risk the truth getting back to Riana now."

"Getting back to her how?"

"The same way my mother found out about our pretend relationship. A friend of hers saw us at Riana's benefit and all of a sudden, my mother thinks we're dating. If I tell my mother it's all for show, who's to say that information won't take the same path back to Riana?"

Allison sighed. She could see his point, but she had to ask, "What happens when all this is over?" She might as well have asked the question of herself. How far was she willing to take her relationship with Zach when she knew it wouldn't last? "I'd hate for Caroline to get her hopes up."

"She won't. She knows me too well. I'm not the kind of guy who does forever."

Allison knew that, too, only she kept forgetting…. Every time he touched her. Every time he looked at her like he was now, with a hint of loneliness and longing hidden behind his eyes, as if waiting, *hoping* she would prove him wrong.

For years after that sledding accident in Flagstaff her father would tell the story of how Allison had conquered the hill, how she'd sluiced through the slaloms, and how she had broken world records.

"And her collarbone," her mother would always interject after blaming Allison for all her nonexistent gray hairs. "I still don't know why you climbed that mountain in the first place."

But her father had known, and the two of them would share a look and whisper, "Because it was there."

Her father had always encouraged her to reach high, to jump far, to never look down. Long before cartoon Dora, he'd called her "Allison the Adventurer." She'd lost some of that sense of adventure when she lost her father and longed to reclaim that part of her personality once more, but was she really up for this? Was she ready to take on a man like Zach?

Chapter Eight

Had anyone asked, Allison would have sworn Zach Wilder in a designer suit and tie was as gorgeous as the guy could get. She'd had plenty of chances, day after day, to take in the way the tailored shirts outlined his wide shoulders before narrowing to tuck inside at his waist. How his thin leather belt encircled a flat stomach. How the cut of his trousers emphasized his long-legged strides. But when she opened the door to her sister's townhouse Saturday morning, she found out how greatly she'd underestimated the power of cotton.

Zach stood on the small landing, looking good enough in casual clothes to leave her speechless. The black T-shirt showcased a pair of biceps that told her skipping workouts at the gym wasn't a common occurrence. The thin material skimmed over washboard abs and disappeared into the waistband of faded denim jeans that molded to his body with the kind of perfection an ad agency would die for.

Hoping he'd chalk up her slack-jawed staring to surprise, Allison asked, "Zach! What are you doing here?"

His dark brows rose as he stepped inside the living room. "We had an appointment, remember? To go over the different options available for your sister's alarm system."

After lunch with Caroline the other day, Zach had brought up the security system again with an offer to put Bethany's initial walk-through on the schedule for the weekend. "I remember..." Her voice trailed off when she saw the toolbox he carried with as much ease as his usual briefcase. "I just didn't expect you to be the one to come out."

Zach shrugged. "This is what I do. It's my job."

His *job* was overseeing multimillion dollar accounts like Collins Jewelers. Pulling in high profile commercial clients was how Zach had made a name for himself at Knox and achieved the success that was so important to him. Selling her sister a system for her tiny townhome wouldn't mean anything to Zach Wilder, Salesman of the Year. But his being there meant everything to Allison.

Something of what she was feeling must have shown in her expression before Zach jerked his gaze away to focus on Bethany's living room. "I like to keep up with the latest residential systems, and I don't get out into the field too often anymore," he said, a hint of defensiveness reminding her of how he'd sent Brad to help with the baby furniture, how he'd dismissed his efforts to help Sylvia. Hiding behind work and refusing to acknowledge any kind of personal interest. "Installs always go more smoothly if a thorough walk-through is done first. I'll check the crawl space in the attic, see how much wiring we'll need and find the best places for the control box."

He could give any excuse, any rational explanation he wanted, but deep down, Allison knew. He was doing this for her, for her sister, because he cared. Maybe he couldn't admit it, but actions spoke louder than words, and everything Zach wasn't saying was working its way into her heart.

"Well," Bethany cleared her throat as she stepped into the room, "you'll get even more practice when you get your hands on Allison's system."

"Thank you, Bethany." Hoping her face wasn't as red as she feared, Allison made quick work of the introductions.

Her sister wasn't the type for suggestive banter, but Bethany's expression was a little too innocent, and Allison wondered how much of her attraction to Zach her sister was picking up on. As much as she wanted to talk about her growing feelings for Zach, the attraction was too new, her own emotions still caught on that *should she/shouldn't she* brink. And after everything that had happened with Kevin, Bethany would likely disapprove of a relationship with Zach. It might even add to the strain on their relationship, something Allison would have to give serious consideration.

Stepping back into salesman mode, Zach said, "I'd recommend our top-of-the-line residential system. It has monitors on the doors and windows and a key chain remote that will activate the alarm. It sounds complicated, but I can go over the details and—"

Bethany held up a silencing hand. "You're the expert. Allison can let me know what you decide when I get back."

"Get back? Where are you going?" Allison asked. She'd come by to make sure Bethany didn't change her mind about getting the alarm but also to have a chance to spend time with her.

"I figured since you were here and you know more about this stuff than I do…" Her sister shrugged. "I've got some errands to run, but I'll be back later."

Within seconds, Bethany had grabbed her purse off the white wicker coffee table and was out the door. Silence fell once she left, and Zach glanced at Allison, his eyebrows raised in question. "Something I said?"

Years ago, the first apartment Bethany shared with Gage had been as familiar as Allison's own. She knew where everything belonged... More importantly, *she* knew where she belonged.

Now, without her sister there, she felt as much of a stranger as Zach.

"Something I did," she admitted. Was Bethany ever going to give her the chance to make up for the distance and mistakes of the past? She'd thought after the day they went shopping and worked together to arrange the furniture in the nursery, she and Bethany would keep growing closer. Instead, their relationship had stalled. No waves currently rocked the boat, but they were merely drifting and going nowhere.

"Hey." Zach set down his toolbox and lifted a hand to tilt her face away from the closed door. Her skin tingled at his touch, and Allison read the question in his eye. But Zach being Zach, he didn't ask the obvious. He simply said, "You okay?"

Allison felt a rush of gratitude. She didn't want to discuss the distance between her and her sister. She didn't even want to think about it right then, and she couldn't have hoped for a better distraction. "Yeah, I'm good. But not as good as you," she added with a glance at his toolbox. She'd never pictured this working-class side of him, but it looked at home on him. And almost as comfortable as the jeans and T-shirt and shadow of beard darkening his jaw. "I can't wait to see you in action."

"How quickly you forget, Allison. I'd say you've already seen me in action at least twice now."

Allison gave a startled laugh. She didn't know if Zach was purposely trying to charm her out of her disappointment in

Bethany's leaving, but like the casual clothes, she wanted to see more of this playful side of him. So after giving him the tour of the house, she settled in to watch him work like some kind of tool belt bunny. "Was it a big change for you, going from working in the field to being in the office?"

"It was, but at the same time, I was ready for it. More than ready." Zach worked as he talked, measuring and making notes on the best locations for running the wires and installing the contacts along the front door jamb. "I'd put in for a few promotions, and the customer service position came open first. I was only there for a few years before the sales position became available. I've been in sales longer than those two positions combined."

"Yeah, but you love sales."

"I do." He hesitated and dropped the measuring tape into his toolbox before meeting her gaze. "But that hasn't stopped me from going after another promotion."

Allison was still recovering from the thought of Zach walking away from a job she knew he loved when he added, "I'm up for VP of sales. The board is supposed to make its decision in the next two weeks. Winning the Collins account would give me the edge over the competition."

"VP? But that's a *management* position," she pointed out, unable to keep the surprise from her voice.

"Yeah, it is. Let me guess," he said, "you think I'd be *good* at it."

She thought he'd hate it. Zach Wilder stuck behind a desk, evaluating salespeople who likely wouldn't have either the drive or talent he possessed? He'd go nuts not being able to go after every lead himself. "Do *you* think you'll be good at it?"

"It's a step up, and that is always a move in the right direction," he said without a hint of the doubts she felt. "When I was still installing, I didn't know if I'd be any good at customer service. But I worked hard, learning everything I could. Same thing happened when I moved into sales, and it'll happen again with the VP position."

"I suppose," Allison agreed halfheartedly.

But what did she know? She wouldn't have pictured Zach as the kind of guy who worked with his hands, but it was easy to imagine him with a drill in his hand, confident in every move, and Allison couldn't pull her gaze away. She followed him from room to room under the guise of understanding the system, but security was the last thing on her mind. Nothing about her attraction to Zach could be called playing it safe.

Especially when the promotion would mean Zach moving to the corporate office in San Francisco.

"So you'll be leaving..."

"No," he answered quickly, making Allison wonder what he might have heard in her voice. "I'd be overseeing the sales teams in Vegas, L.A. and here, so Phoenix would stay my base of operations for now."

"I see," Allison said truthfully.

She saw Zach taking on new responsibilities that included a tri-state commute. He'd be stretched so thin, no relationship would stand a chance. But he'd already told her he didn't do forever. The news of the promotion wasn't any cause for Allison's stomach to tie in knots or for loss to sweep through her forcefully enough to leave her feeling hollow inside. It was better this way, right? To push off the edge of that hill, eyes wide open to what lay ahead? With Zach, there was no chance of being blindsided. *Any* relationship would be temporary, and when the time came, they'd both be ready to move on.

"This is the last room," Allison told Zach as she opened the door to the secondary bedroom. "It's the nursery. Or will be once it's finished."

"Looks ready to me," Zach said as he eyed the dresser, changing table and crib.

"It takes more than baby furniture to make a nursery. It's far too bland and boring as it is," she said with a wave of her hand. "You need cartoon character murals and bright colors everywhere."

"Hmm, I get the feeling Bethany wasn't too thrilled with that idea."

She laughed. "That's because she's seen me decorate and knows I have absolutely no artistic ability." Allison said the words without a false sense of modesty or in the hope of gaining a compliment.

"Right up there with ceramics, huh?" Zach asked, thinking of the lopsided coffee cup she used at work.

She scrunched her nose in thought. "I'd say not quite as good as the ceramics."

He watched as she smoothed a wrinkle out of the bunny sheets. "I don't get it, Allison."

The dreamy smile drifted from her face and wariness crept in. "Get what?"

"You. And all the hobbies you waste time on."

"They're not a waste of time," she protested.

"They are if you don't enjoy them. And don't tell me you do. You aren't the kind of person who's going to get all excited about a straight line of needlepoint."

"I probably would considering I've never managed a straight line," she muttered.

Ignoring that, he pressed, "I know family's important to you, and you want to reconnect with your sister. But...I've watched you work. I've seen the excitement, the spark in your eyes when you're on to something. And I've seen that light die when you talk about moving on to another temp job."

"That's not true," Allison protested, her voice weak. But when Zach didn't answer, letting silence speak for him, her shoulders slouched on a sigh, and she sank onto the narrow window seat. "My sister and I were so close growing up... Do you have any siblings?"

"No. Only child," Zach said as he sat beside her. As a kid, he'd often longed for a brother or sister only to later realize being an only child was for the best. Another kid would have simply given his father another reason to complain.

"Growing up, Bethany and I were more than sisters. We were best friends. I never cared about fitting in at school or worried about having someone to sit with at lunch because I always had Bethany. But now..." Allison lifted her hands helplessly. "It's hard to remember that we were ever that close, and I need to prove to her that I've changed. That family matters more to me than any job ever could."

"Don't you think you've proved that by now with the temp jobs?"

"Then why is there still such a barrier between us?"

"Maybe that's not why she's really upset. Maybe it's something else entirely."

"I don't suppose you can tell me what that something else might be?"

Even though he didn't hear any sarcasm behind Allison's question, Zach wondered what the hell he thought he was doing handing out advice on family harmony. Like he was some kind of expert! Allison would be better off taking her cues from a fortune cookie. "I don't know. You said you'd always been close.... What changed?"

"My senior year of college, I started seeing this guy. Kevin Hodges. He was smart and ambitious and driven. He understood how much I loved advertising and the goals I'd set for myself."

"What goals?" Zach asked gently as if he knew she hadn't achieved them and had perhaps even guessed that only a traumatic event could have convinced her to give them up.

"To hire on at a big advertising firm, work my way up until I'd made a name for myself before starting my own company." Seeing the surprised lift to Zach eyebrows, she added, "All before I turned thirty."

"Impressive."

"Yeah, Kevin thought so, too. In fact, the idea of starting a business was something we had in common. Something Bethany and I didn't share. She'd taken a few college courses and worked a few jobs in retail, but they were just jobs. What she really wanted was to have a family. She and Gage got married the summer after I graduated."

The wedding was the last time her family had truly been together, and it hurt that those memories were now clouded by Gage and Bethany's separation. A separation Allison didn't understand and Bethany refused to talk about.

"A few weeks after that, Kevin received a job offer for a firm in New York. An old family friend of his father's worked at Barton/Mills, giving Kevin an in most recent grads would die for. He even had his friend ask around to find an opening in the firm for me. It was an entry-level position, but I didn't care. After all, working my way up had always been part of my plan."

She'd been so naïve, so certain hard work would be recognized and rewarded. She'd been completely blind to that fact that some people were willing to succeed at any cost.

"And that's what caused the rift between you and Bethany?" Zach surmised. "She resented you for taking the job in New York when she wanted you to stay here?"

Naturally, Zach, with his belief that personal ties would only hold him back, assumed Bethany had discouraged her far-flung dreams of success, but he was wrong. "No, she was thrilled for me. She might not have understood my goals, but she supported me every step of the way. When I told her I wasn't sure I was ready to take such a big step, Bethany was the one to tell me I didn't dare turn down a chance of a life-time opportunity."

"So you went to the Big Apple and…"

"And I loved it. The energy, the fast pace, the constant motion. I thought it was amazing, if you can believe that."

"I can." Allison had that same energy humming beneath her skin when she wasn't busy trying to suppress it. He could easily imagine her amid the crowds in New York, just like he could imagine her working her way up in an ad firm. Advertising was big business but with a creative flair that fit Allison to a T. "I can picture you hitting the sidewalk ready to take on anything and anyone. I bet you can even do that two-fingered whistle."

"You mean like this?" Placing her thumb and forefinger against her lips, she let loose an ear-piercing whistle bound to stop any cab within a mile radius.

Wincing in mock pain, Zach said, "That's the one."

"I learned a lot in New York." Her smile fell away, and Zach knew some of those lessons had been painful ones. "Unfortunately, I forgot a lot of the things I'd learned here."

"Like what?"

"Like birthdays and anniversaries and holidays. I forgot how important family is, and I'm still not sure how I let it happen. When I left for New York, I made all kinds of promises. I'd email every day and call once a week and spend all my vacations on trips back home. I meant every word, too. But I underestimated how quickly I would get pulled into a desire to prove myself, to succeed."

Zach knew exactly what Allison was talking about. How addictive the thrill of the chase could be. But while he lived for that chase, felt it pulsing through his veins like a shot of adrenaline, talking about it left Allison drained of energy. Sorrow bowed her shoulders, and Zach once again realized that was what families did. Burdened you with so much guilt you didn't have a chance to reach for your dreams.

"The emails dropped to once a week, phone calls to once a month. And somehow, those trips home never happened."

"How long were you in New York?"

"Three years."

"Why did you leave?"

"I had promised my sister I would help plan a surprise party for my dad's sixtieth birthday. Of course, my help ended up being nothing more than a five-second phone call or two, telling Bethany to do whatever she thought best. And then, the firm had a huge client fall into our laps. A major cosmetic company fired their advertising company. They were prepared to give our company the contract if we could wow them with half a dozen potential ads by the following week."

"So you canceled your trip home."

"Close. I told Bethany I would fly in for the party and then turn around and head home. For my sister, that was the last straw. We got into a huge fight, yelling and calling each other names. Things we didn't do as kids. Finally, I told her if she really thought I was so selfish and so self-centered, she probably wouldn't want me at the party, and I hung up."

"People say things when they're angry, but you shouldn't be so hard on yourself. It's not that bad—"

"No, it wasn't that bad." Allison pushed to her feet, agitation carrying her across the room to the crib she and Bethany had picked out together. "The bad part came later," she whispered, "when Bethany called me at work the next week. I was ten minutes from pitching my idea to the cosmetic company, and I wasn't about to let her spoil my moment of triumph with all her negative opinions about my job and my priorities. So I didn't take the call. I went in and I gave the pitch of my life. The print campaign, the commercials, everything was exactly what the client was looking for, and we won the account. We were all headed out for a night on the town to celebrate when I remembered Bethany's call. I called her back, ready to gloat about the amazing job I'd done, and that's when she told me. Our father had had a heart attack. I flew out as soon as I could, but it was too late. *I* was too late. He was already gone. I keep waiting, *hoping* Bethany will forgive me. Because...maybe—maybe then I'll be able to forgive myself."

Her hands gripped the crib railing like a lifeline; a single soft sound of sorrow escaped her threat. The muted sob threatened to break Zach's heart, and without thinking, he took three quick strides and pulled Allison into his arms. He'd never been the comforting type, had never dealt with a woman's tears before.

But this wasn't any woman. This was Allison. Tough, smart, wisecracking Allison. Only he was starting to realize how much her bold personality hid the vulnerability inside. The urge to wipe away her sadness, to solve all her problems hit Zach with a desire he'd never experienced outside of work, along with an insecurity he hadn't felt since he was a kid. Helpless, he struggled for words and found nothing.

What was wrong with him that he couldn't say *something?* Couldn't offer some sort of consolation? Was he that heartless? That empty inside? "Allie—"

Her head lifted at the sound of his voice. One look into her damp green eyes, and no words were necessary. He brushed his mouth against hers, his lips and tongue conveying everything he thought he didn't know how to say.

I'm so sorry.

It's not your fault.

You need to forgive yourself.

And as the tension eased from her body and the tears dried from her cheeks, Zach sensed she heard every word in her answering kiss.

* * *

Zach finished the last of his notes for the security system by rote. Fortunately, he was so familiar with the system, he no longer had to think about what he was doing. A good thing since his thoughts and emotions were tied up in a knot that couldn't be untangled as easily as separating the right color wire.

He and Allison had been tap dancing back and forth over the line of business versus pleasure since before they started working together, but this time he feared finding his way back wouldn't be so easy. Like in the Harrison Ford movies he'd loved as a kid, Zach felt the ground behind him starting to crumble beneath his feet, giving him no choice but to hold on to his hat and jump into an unknown future. But he wasn't so sure he had the adventurer's uncanny ability to survive the landing unscathed.

He and Allison had kissed before, but desire, need, even frustration had fueled those embraces. Today was different. Desire and need were still present and accounted for; Allison's proximity as she followed him from room to room, her curious and appreciative gaze marking his every move, guaranteed that.

But more dangerous and far less easily defined—or easily dismissed—emotions had underscored their last kiss. Pulling Allison into his arms hadn't been about wanting her as much as it had been about wanting to hold her. To comfort her.

He wasn't quite sure where that kind of longing had come from, only that it pretty much scared the hell out of him. He wasn't the comforting type. That he'd even tried warned Zach he was in much further over his head than he'd imagined.

He heard footsteps in the hallway, but it was Bethany, not Allison, who stepped into the nursery. "Allison said you're almost done."

"I have everything we'll need for the install. I can go over the system if you'd like, but Allison has it down."

"No, that's okay. But thanks for the offer and your help."

"Allison's the one who really deserves the thanks, not me."

"Yeah, well." Bethany shrugged, but he wasn't buying the nonchalant reaction. Keeping her distance from Allison wasn't as easy as Bethany wanted it to seem. "Thanks."

"You're welcome," he said as she led him down the hall.

Allison was nowhere in sight, which Zach told himself was a relief although it didn't stop him from pausing at the front door and waiting on the chance she might come out from the back of the house. When she didn't show, he told Bethany, "We may have to drill some small holes in the drywall to run wires to the alarm. You should be able to touch them up pretty easily, but your sister has it in her mind to repaint the nursery anyway. Knowing Allison, though, I'm betting she's really bad at it."

Bethany groaned. "She's awful. She tried painting a red accent wall in her condo only the paint ran so badly it looked like blood was oozing from the drywall!"

"Yeah, that's Allison for you. I've never known such a smart, talented woman who takes such pride in failing. It's almost like she's afraid to succeed." A flash of something— admission, guilt—leapt in Bethany's eyes, and he could feel her staring after him as he jogged down the steps to the driveway. He didn't know if his words had any effect on Bethany, but they'd knocked him for a loop.

Knowing Allison... That phrase kept ringing in his head. He *did* know Allison. And he was getting to know her better every time they talked, every moment they spent together.

But getting to know a woman, especially one he worked with, was *not* part of the plan.

And what about holding her when she cried? His conscience jeered. What about feeling the curves of her body pressed against him as he kissed her? Where did *that* fit into the plan?

It didn't fit, he insisted. *Allison* didn't fit.

But despite the reminder, he couldn't forget how perfect she felt in his arms, her head tucked beneath his chin, her cheek against chest... Almost as if that spot had been empty his entire life and he'd simply been waiting for her to find the place where she belonged.

Chapter Nine

"You're going to do great, Zach." Allison flashed a bright smile as the last PowerPoint slide flashed across the screen.

She'd been practicing that smile all week. Ever since the day at Bethany's when she'd fallen apart in Zach's arms. When he'd silently held her and let his touch, his kiss, the tenderness in his gaze soothe her the way words never could. Wrapped in his embrace she'd felt safe and protected and never wanted to leave. She never wanted to let go.

He never stopped resenting me for ruining the life he could have had.

Sooner or later, he's going to realize you're only holding him back.

She *had* to let him go.

When the time came, Allison would wish Zach well and send him off with a smile. It didn't matter if her heart was breaking. Or that she wanted to erase every bad memory he had as a child and show him how family, how *love*, meant far more than football or fame. She couldn't change the hard lessons that made him the man he was now—a man who was going places, a man who'd spent his entire career building on opportunities to move up and move on.

In the end, whether it came when he won the promotion or when he obtained some other far-reaching goal, he would leave her behind.

Zach hit the conference room lights and gave her a rueful smile. "Come on, Allie. Don't start pulling punches now."

It was the day before Zach's meeting with James Collins, and Daryl had asked for a preview of the presentation. Something, Zach had confessed, his boss had never requested before. He hadn't admitted it, but Allison knew how much Daryl's suddenly hands-on approach bothered him.

"I think you know me better than that," she responded. "I'm not the type to hold back, and the presentation is far more personalized now."

"But you think it needs more."

Knowing she was on slippery ground, Allison chose her steps carefully. "I think the break-in that happened when you were younger gives you an experience most people don't have. Plus you're a great salesman, but what matters more is that you're a great guy. You care about people. Not just your family, but people you barely know like my sister and an old lady in Sun City."

"Like James Collins is going to care about any of that."

Maybe not. But Allison did. She cared too much—about the man Zach was and the boy he'd once been. She understood why it was so hard for him to open up and put himself on the line. The risk of rejection was too great after the way his father had emotionally turned his back before Zach was even born. But if he would crack that door just a little then…

What exactly? Did she really think Zach might fall for her…like she'd fallen for him?

"Allison? Are you okay?"

"Yeah. Sure. Fine." Allison swallowed. As fine as a woman who'd fallen in love with the last man on earth she should fall for could be. "Zach, I—" She heard a sudden pounding and, for a moment, feared her fool heart was ready to jump out of her chest and spill itself all over the conference room table.

Instead, Martha opened the door and stuck her head inside. "Allison, you have a call. It's your sister."

More than eager to escape, she tossed an apology over her shoulder to Zach as she nearly ran from the conference room down the hall to their shared office. She closed the door behind her and leaned against it briefly. She hadn't almost told Zach she loved him, had she? To even *think* the words was bad, but if she said them out loud, there'd be no taking them back. No hiding from her feelings.

Her heart still pounding from the close call, Allison picked up the phone. "Hey, Bethie," she said, falling back on a nickname she hadn't used in years. "Is everything okay?"

"I'm starting to make a habit of this, aren't I?" Her sister gave a rough, pained laugh. "Calling you at work with problems. I know you hate that—"

"No," Allison interrupted, shoving her own problems aside, "you can call me anytime. Nothing is more important to me than being here if you need me."

Silence followed her promise, a gap Allison filled with worry. Did Bethany believe she'd keep her word? Would her sister start to lower the walls between them and let Allison help?

"Gage wants a divorce."

Bethany's softly whispered words seemed to suck the air from Allison's lungs. Once, when she was five, she'd slipped off a jungle gym. The fall had knocked the wind out of her, leaving her lying on the ground, struggling for air.

She felt the same way now... On a sudden gasp, her breath

rushed back in and out again, her words topping hurricane speed as she demanded, "He said that?"

Allison had known her sister's marriage had hit a rough spot; a husband didn't move out on his pregnant wife if everything was smooth sailing. But she'd never thought, never considered, they wouldn't get back together.

"I thought if I gave him enough time," her sister was saying woodenly, "he'd forgive me. He'd have to... But he's not. He won't."

"Bethany, I am so sorry. I don't know what else to say. How could Gage do this?"

"It's not his fault. It's my fault. All my fault—I don't know what I'm going to do, Allie." For the first time, her sister's voice trembled, hinting at the emotion bottled up inside. "I don't know how I'm going to raise this baby alone."

"You are *not* alone," Allison insisted. "I'm here for you, Bethany, for anything you need. And you know how excited Mom is. Once that baby of yours is born, he or she won't be able to sneeze without grandma saying 'God bless you.'"

It wasn't much of a joke, but Bethany's watery laugh gave Allison the small glimmer of hope she'd been waiting for since coming home.

Sitting at Bethany's kitchen table, Allison struggled with the helplessness and anger twisting inside her. Her sister was quiet, her eyes red-rimmed and bloodshot, but she hadn't cried a single tear in front of Allison. Nor had she said one bad word about Gage or offered an explanation for their split.

"I can't believe Gage would do this."

Allison had always liked Gage, had grown to love him as the brother she'd never had. She knew she was supposed to be understanding and supportive, but she didn't understand any of this...least of all Bethany's reaction.

"I know you guys were having problems—" Gage's

moving out couldn't mean anything else, but beyond that, Allison didn't have a clue "—but I thought for sure you'd get back together, that he'd come to his senses."

Swallowing hard, Bethany said, "He has."

"You're telling me divorcing his pregnant wife is the sensible decision?" Allison demanded, incredulous. Reaching out to take her sister's hands, she pleaded, "Talk to me, Bethany. The two of you were so happy. What happened? Is there someone else?"

For a moment, Allison feared Bethany would maintain her stubborn silence, the impenetrable distance the years had put between them. When she pulled her hands away, Allison's heart sank. Only instead of pushing away from the table or refusing to answer the questions, Bethany cradled her stomach and murmured, "I guess you could say that."

Feeling like her mental shoelaces were tied together, Allison's thoughts tripped over one another as she tried to make sense of what her sister was saying. "You mean Gage left because of the baby? Because the baby is…" Unable to finish the sentence, her words trailed off.

Giving her an affronted glance, Bethany interjected, "Gage's. The baby is Gage's, Allison."

"Sorry! I'm sorry. When I asked if there was someone else, I meant if Gage was seeing someone else, but then you said the baby and— Obviously, I'm confused. Why would Gage want to divorce you because of the baby?"

"When we first got married, Gage wanted to wait before having kids, and I was okay with that. I would have liked to try right away, but I agreed that we should have some time alone first. But then one year went by, and another, and another, and we were still waiting. Before long, everywhere I went, everywhere I looked, there were babies. Kids on swing sets at the park, kids in strollers on the track, movie stars adopting kids or having two or three of their own. Everyone seemed to have a baby except for me.

"It had been a few months since I'd talked to Gage about having kids. He'd seemed stressed about something he wouldn't discuss, and at the time, I told myself I didn't want to add to his troubles. But then July rolled around. Another year, another birthday, and I didn't want to wait any longer. The timing might not have been perfect, but timing's never perfect. So, stressed out or not, I told Gage I thought it was time for us to have kids."

"What happened?"

"I don't know. I've gone over that moment again and again, and I still don't know what happened. At first, he froze, and then he just exploded. It was like some action adventure movie where they use slow motion leading up to the big moment. He didn't want kids. Not now, not ever, not up for discussion."

"That doesn't even sound like Gage." Bethany's husband had a temper, but he worked hard to keep it under control. Sometimes, Allison thought Gage was almost *too* controlled.

"I know. I couldn't believe what he was saying. I *didn't* believe it. I told myself he had cold feet, and eventually, I'd convince him. I'd wear him down until he saw how great a dad he would be, and I'd have everything I wanted. And then Dad died, and well, I guess I went a little crazy."

"We all did," Allison agreed, recalling her mother's and her own grief.

Bethany offered a self-deprecating smile. "Maybe. But we didn't all go off our birth control without telling our husbands."

"Oh, Bethany."

Throwing her arms wide, Bethany said, "Go ahead. Yell at me. Tell me how I deceived and betrayed Gage's trust and that I don't deserve his forgiveness."

"Is that what he said?"

Her arms collapsing back to her sides like a marionette with broken strings, Bethany said, "Gage didn't say a thing. Not one word. He left and was gone for days. When he came home, it was to pack up his things and move out. We haven't had a single meaningful conversation since. So now I have the baby I've always wanted, but I've lost my husband. I guess you can't have everything after all."

"I'm so sorry, Bethany. And I'm sorry I wasn't here when Dad died."

Her sister shook her head like she did every time Allison brought up that horrible time. "I don't want to talk about it."

"We have to, Bethany." Hating to push her sister now, Allison said, "We need to get through this. I want us to be close again, like we were before. We were more than sisters. We were *friends*. You could use a friend right now, and—and so could I."

At first, Allison feared Bethany was going to continue to shut her out, but then her sister leaned forward. She braced her elbows on the table and stared at her folded hands as if they held a crystal ball. Only instead of showing the future, she was seeing the past. "I was at the house when Dad had his heart attack. I called 911, tried to keep him comfortable and to keep Mom calm. She rode with him in the ambulance, and I drove behind them.

"When we got to the hospital, all I could think was that I wanted to see him, as if that might somehow make everything all right. They wouldn't let us into his room right away, and when they did, well, I think it was because they knew he wasn't going to make it.

"I was sitting with him, trying to find the words to say goodbye." As Bethany lifted her gaze, Allison read the devastation, the sorrow, and the bitter resentment her sister had bottled for months. "Dad opened his eyes, looked right at me...and asked for you."

An echo of the pain her sister must have felt pierced Allison's heart. She hadn't been at her father's side when he needed her... Hadn't had the chance to take his hand, to look in his eyes, to tell him she loved him one more time... "Oh, Bethany—"

Her sister shoved away from the table. Fueled by the fury she'd finally unleashed, Bethany lashed out. "I don't even know why I was surprised. Ever since you moved away, it was always about you!" She flung a hand out, and Allison flinched as if her sister had made actual contact. "It wasn't a holiday, wasn't a celebration unless *Allison* came home. It didn't matter that I was there for every birthday, every anniversary..."

"No! Bethany, no! It wasn't like that!"

"How would you know? *You* weren't here."

"And that's why Dad had to ask for me! It wasn't because he wanted me at his side more than he wanted you there. He could count on you being there. I was the one who missed those holidays, those weekly dinners. I was the one—the one who missed my chance to say goodbye." Her voice broke on the word, the ragged edges leaving her throat raw and aching with unshed tears. "I regret that more than you can imagine, but there's nothing I can do to change it."

Pulling her shoulders back, Bethany regained the calm, stoic demeanor Allison had faced since she'd returned home. "No, there isn't."

Allison stepped inside her condo emotionally exhausted. Not since her father's funeral had she felt so wrung out. But she'd asked for this, hadn't she? She'd wanted to know the real reason why Bethany wouldn't forgive her, and now she knew. She knew...

He asked for you… You weren't there…

And oh, how that hurt! Getting her sister to let go of all the bitterness and anger was supposed to help, but Allison hadn't guessed, couldn't have imagined that the process would be so slow and painful. Like peeling bandages off wounds covered too long, Bethany's words had ripped away pieces of her soul, and Allison didn't know how that hurt could ever heal.

She moved through her condo in slow motion, fumbling as she changed out of the outfit she'd worn to work as if trying to make someone else's limbs move, as if trying to guide someone else's fingers through the necessary steps of unzipping and unbuttoning clothes. When the doorbell rang as she was pulling on a T-shirt and pair of sweats, Allison ignored the sound. Whoever it was would give up in a minute. They'd figure she wasn't home and leave her in peace—

But when the bell rang again, Allison dragged her feet into the living room. She was reaching for the handle when a deep, oh-so-familiar voice said, "Allison? Open the door."

"Go away, Zach," she whispered, crossing her arms over her chest as she backed away.

The silencing coming from outside lasted so long, she started to think he'd actually listened to her for once. Finally, though, Zach replied, "I'm not leaving, so you might as well let me in."

With raw emotions so close to the surface, the last thing she should do was open the door. And yet she took one step closer. Then another. "I'm fine." The words were a last, desperate attempt and, considering the watery sound of tears in her voice, not a very convincing one.

"Allie…" His soft voice carried through the closed panel. "Let me in."

Dropping her head against the door, Allison admitted defeat. She couldn't resist, even though letting Zach in would mean so much more than simply opening the door. She might as well put a welcome mat on her heart and invite him to trample all over it.

"Your neighbors are going to wonder about the suspicious-looking guy lingering outside your door all night."

All night... "You've got the meeting with James Collins in the morning," she said as she opened the door. "You should be at work polishing the presentation until it's perfect."

"It is perfect," Zach argued. "Daryl was impressed. He says it's a home run—thanks to you."

"Thanks to me?"

"It was your idea to narrow the focus and limit the technical details. Not to mention the work you did on the PowerPoint. I wasn't about to take all the credit."

"You could have," she whispered. Kevin had done so much worse, but Zach wasn't Kevin. After getting to know him, Allison wasn't sure what made her think the two men were anything alike to begin with. Zach had a work ethic and integrity Kevin Hodges completely lacked.

"No way. I've always worked alone, but you've made me realize there are some things I don't mind sharing."

Sharing his success... For a man like Zach, that might be as close as he would get to opening his heart.

Tears burned her eyes, but before a single one could fall, Zach pulled her into his arms. Resting her head against his chest, Allison breathed in the subtle scent of his cologne and let the warmth of his body soothe the bruised and broken edges of her soul. His palm ran up and down the length of her spine, and Allison's tears eased with each caress until they finally subsided. Gradually, she became aware of his hand resting at the curve of her hip and the steady, hypnotic beat of his heart against her cheek. Any minute now, she knew she'd have to unclench the back of his shirt from her fists and step away even though all she really wanted was to be closer. Much closer...

Because you haven't already acted like a total fool, you might as well throw yourself at him.

Her face heating at the thought, Allison ducked her head and pulled away. "Oh, how you must hate this," she said with a watery laugh.

Zach lifted her chin and quirked an eyebrow at her as he brushed the tears from her cheeks. "Which part?"

"Um, the overly emotional woman crying all over you—again—because of her personal problems part?"

"Oh, well, that wasn't so bad. Especially if it helped." The concern was back as he asked, "Did it? Enough for me to ask how things went with you and Bethany without risk of more tears?"

"Yes, it helped, but no promises on the no-more-tears angle," she warned.

"I'll take my chances."

"I've been waiting for an opening to make things up to Bethany, but I never wanted this." Wandering over to the couch, she sank into the cushion and pulled a pillow into her lap; she hugged it against her chest as if the soft comfort might somehow protect her aching heart. "What's worse is that I still don't know if it changed anything. If she's ever going to completely forgive me."

"She will."

Certainty cemented Zach's words as he sat beside her, and Allison clung to them like an anchor even as she asked, "How can you be so sure?"

"Because," he said, his expression as tender as his touch as he brushed a lock of hair away from her cheek, "if she's anything like you, family means everything. She's still angry, but she won't stay that way forever. Not when she knows how much you care about her."

She cared just as much about Zach, but she couldn't tell him. Words would only push him away, but she knew how to draw him closer. Leaning forward, she brushed her lips against his, her touch as feather light as his was against her cheek. But the combination of heat and breath added to the intensity, to the desire that had been building for weeks.

Allison leaned back, wanting, needing to see that he wanted this as much as she did. Wanted her as much as she wanted him. The catch in his breathing, the blue-black darkening of his eyes and tension tightening his entire body convinced her. His hands skimmed down her back, coming to rest at her waist, fingers rhythmically tightening on her hips, and she let the pillow fall to the floor, exchanging cool softness for the warmth and strength of his shoulders. She inhaled his cologne, the now-familiar scent leaving her restless and aching.

In the back of her mind, warning flares fired off, one right after another in a mental SOS Allison fought to ignore. She was too emotional, too vulnerable for this to happen now. Every last reserve was stretched to the breaking point, shoring up her defenses to keep her heart from bleeding out over her sister's accusations. She couldn't withstand another assault, especially not the sensual, seductive kind Zach was waging.

You can't have everything... Bethany's words rang in her head, and Allison knew they were true. *Everything* would have been Zach in her arms for more than one night; *everything* would have been knowing he was falling for her as hard and as fast as she was falling for him.

She couldn't have everything, but she could have tonight, and she could hope that would be enough.

She sank into his kiss, letting the heat wash over her, soothing her emotional aches until the idea of leaving his arms was as chilling as the thought of jumping from a hot spring into an icy lake. She wanted to stay forever; weightless, boneless and buoyed by gentle, easy eddies.

Allison wasn't sure when the current changed, when the blood in her veins picked up speed, when the white-water rapids of desire rushed through her. Zach's grip on her hip tightened as he stretched full length beside her. His tongue teased her upper lip, tracing and tasting the sensitive flesh without giving into her demands for more. Unwilling to simply drift along any longer, Allison shifted her weight, pressing her breasts to his chest, her legs straddling his. And just like that, the anchor holding back his need gave way.

Catching her face in his hands, he surged into the kiss. A sensual thrill raced through her. She'd known Zach would be like this—as focused and dedicated to pleasure as he was to business. His breath was ragged in her ear as he trailed kisses along her collarbone left bare by the wide neck of her T-shirt. He followed the delicate line to the hollow of her throat and between her breasts where her heart pounded a crazy, wild beat.

She gasped his name as she fisted her hands in the starched crispness of his shirt. Answering the need in her voice, Zach cupped her breast. Her flesh swelled beneath the heat of his touch, her nipple tightening into his palm, the friction of super-soft cotton almost as arousing as the tug and pull of skin against skin. Almost.

Pure pleasure keeping her doubts at bay, Allison rose to her knees on either side of Zach's hips. She grasped for the hem of her shirt, ready to pull it over her head, but his hands got in the way. Not in a tangle of material as he tried to strip away her clothes but as he reached up to rub a thumb beneath her eye. His touch left a damp trail against her cheek, a reminder of the tears she'd cried. Running mascara and messy makeup was normally a morning after concern, not a problem the night before, but Allison didn't think it was raccoon eyes that had Zach slowing down.

But without the rush of passion, hurt and regret crowded

in, burning the back of her throat and stinging her eyes like bitter acid. *Not yet,* she thought, almost desperately. *Please, not yet.* She wasn't ready to face reality, not if she could live in the fantasy of Zach's arms for a little longer.

He pushed into a sitting position, but Allison took advantage of an arrangement that left them eye to eye, mouth to mouth...

"Allie."

She felt him speak, giving her name taste and texture instead of merely sound, and she answered in kind, whispering against his lips. "Yes?"

"I'm not taking advantage of you."

"No," she said in quick agreement. "You're not."

His rough laugh reverberated through her entire body. "I mean, I'm *not* taking advantage of you." He caught her face in his hands, holding her gaze when she might have ducked away from the compassion and understanding she saw there. "You've had an emotional evening. I don't want you to regret this in the morning."

It was that protective streak of his, the one he tried so hard to hide. Taking control of his actions and taking possession of her heart. "I don't—"

"Don't what?"

Breaking every rule, every promise she'd made to herself, Allison whispered, "I don't want you to go."

Settling her against his chest, Zach murmured, "I'm right here."

Right here. Right now.

With her head pressed to his heart, Allison counted every beat and measured every breath as she tried to remember everything about a moment she already knew wouldn't last.

Chapter Ten

As the door to James Collins's office opened, Zach turned at the sound but the man he was expecting didn't step through the doorway. If this was another one of Riana Collins's games— Checking his anger, he calmly said, "Hello, Riana. It's good to see you again."

"Is it?" A wry smile tugged her lips as she stepped into the room. The black sweaterdress she wore covered her from neck to knee, but the thin material hugged every impressive curve like an expensive sports car handling a dangerous road. Any smart man would proceed with caution, but cautious men weren't the type to buy sports car, were they?

As Allison pointed out, men bought those cars because of how they made them feel—rich and powerful and sexy.

Riana was all of those things, but she still left Zach cold.

But Allison—Allison turned him on like no woman ever had.

For the first time in his life, he'd spent the night with a woman without *actually* spending the night—some kind of testament when it came to self-control, he was sure. He wasn't sure how long he'd held her on the couch, her body curled into his, before she fell asleep.

With her head cradled against his chest, she'd looked young and fragile, her eyes closed and her lips gently parted. Her quick-thinking, fast-talking personality hid a vulnerability that brought a tenderness and protective side out in him. And whether she knew it or not, Allison had put those newfound instincts to a serious test.

In the early hours of the morning, she'd taken a deep breath, stretched, and shifted closer, her soft, languid body a painful contrast to his own. He'd read the surrender in her still slumberous gaze and knew she wouldn't have resisted. One kiss, one touch, and she would have been his. The tension in his body clamored for release, to take what Allison was offering. But, keeping his promise not to take advantage, he'd urged her into bed, leaving her with nothing more than an innocent kiss...

That had been less than three hours ago, and if he'd dragged himself away to jump through another one of Riana's hoops—

"Relax, Zach," the brunette told him as she picked up on the frustration he'd tried to hide. "My father will be here in a minute. He'd never miss a business meeting. His company is what he lives for."

She waved her hand at the surrounding office, and Zach had to admit, the place all but confirmed her words. The area looked ready for a photo shoot for an architectural magazine. The room combined classic cherrywood in the built-in shelves and enormous desk with modern touches of polished chrome in the lighting, free-form sculptures, black granite floors and state-of-the-art computer system.

Everything was spotless and completely impersonal.

There was nothing to reveal James Collins as anything but a focused, driven businessman.

Still, Zach argued, "I think more than the company matters to your father. At the groundbreaking, he introduced employees who'd been with him for years, decades even, and now they've made the move across country to be here for this new beginning. People don't show that level of a commitment unless they've been treated well. Treated like family."

For a split second, Zach thought he saw something soften in Riana's expression, but then she tossed her head with a laugh. "That's some golden tongue, Zach. You almost had me believing that pitch."

"I know you think my job is all about making a sale, but to me, it's more than that."

Riana raised her eyebrows, her doubt obvious. "Normally, I can pin people down within a few minutes. When we first met, I had you as a man who lived to work, one who'd do anything for his career."

"You were right. That's exactly who I am."

That's who I am.

But Riana's eyes narrowed, still studying him like someone she'd never seen before, and who could blame her? He fought the urge to loosen the tie suddenly strangling him, but he knew it wouldn't help. He rubbed a hand over the back of his neck, uncomfortable in his own skin.

You're a great salesman, but what matters more is that you're a great guy.

Only days ago, he would have sworn nothing meant more to him than being a great salesman. Now, he knew differently. What mattered most was that Allison believed in him. That *she* thought he was a good guy whether he was ready to believe it or not.

Lowering his arm, he told Riana, "But that's not *all* I am."

Riana shook her head with a soft laugh. "I guess not. Not anymore."

"Morning, Zach. Sorry I'm late." With his gaze focused on his phone, James Collins was halfway into the room before he spotted his daughter in his office. "Riana, what—"

His daughter breezed by him with barely a glance. "I was just leaving, Daddy. Zach's all yours."

James glanced back over his shoulder in his daughter's wake, and for a moment, Zach saw what Allison had been telling him all along. James Collins might be a hardened businessman, but he was also a widowed father at a loss with his own daughter. But by the time James looked back at Zach, all confusion had cleared from his expression, and he pierced Zach with a no-nonsense stare.

"Before we start, you should know whatever relationship you have with my daughter will have no bearing on my decision."

"I didn't think it would, but before we start, I should point out that Riana and I don't have any kind of relationship outside of business."

James held his gaze for another moment before offering an abrupt nod and stating, "All right then. Have a seat."

In the years that he'd worked at Knox, Zach had learned to read prospective clients. He knew when a presentation was going well. Forty-five minutes in, the presentation with James Collins was *not* going well.

Not that Collins had given anything away. Seated across the desk from Zach, the man had listened to everything Zach said, responded to his questions, asked a few of his own. But Zach knew the man was nowhere near signing a contract.

You need that personal connection.

Allison's voice whispered through his thoughts. If he wanted her to believe in him, trust in him, then maybe wasn't it time he took that same chance on her?

Hoping he wasn't about to commit professional suicide, Zach said, "The truth is, Mr. Collins, Knox Security is the best around. And I can tell you everything you'd want to know about our motion detectors and pressure sensors, and all the devices designed to keep your jewelry safe. But where I think Knox Security excels is in keeping people safe."

Taking a deep breath and wishing Allison was there with him, he dove into uncharted waters. "That was a major factor for me and my mother when we were looking for a security system after our home was invaded." Zach saw the first flicker of interest in Collins's expression as he briefly explained the break-in. "I hated leaving my mom at home alone after that, but the alarm helped."

"You know," Collins said with a smile, "the first piece of jewelry I ever created was for my mother on Mother's Day. She assured me it was the most beautiful brooch she'd ever seen. Even then I knew it was hideous."

"Must be worth a fortune now."

The older man laughed. "It might have been if it hadn't fallen apart after a few weeks." Collins leaned forward and took another look at the sales folder Allison had prepared. "Tell me more about the silent alarm..."

Allison's cell phone rang once, then fell silent. A quick glance showed Daryl's number illuminated on the screen. Picking up a nearby water glass, she rapped a fork against the side. "Hey, everybody!" she called out, trying to be heard over the sports bar's raucous party atmosphere. "Daryl and Zach are on their way!" A loud cheer followed her announcement. "Everybody hide!"

"Where?" Brett Mitchell called out.

The bar was packed with Knox employees, all gathered to celebrate Zach's now unquestionable victory. It was Daryl's job to get the hero of the hour to the party where Caroline had arranged for appetizers and a cash bar.

"Um…" Allison caught Caroline's eye. The other woman shrugged helplessly, leaving Allison to gaze at two dozen or so of her fellow employees. "Okay, everybody face away from the entrance and try to look shifty. Like people who would *never* work at a security company!"

A round of laughter followed her announcement, but many of the partygoers did turn to face the back patio. Less than a minute later, Allison heard a party horn blow, the signal for Zach's arrival, and she and everyone else turned to shout, "Surprise!"

Laughing, Zach made a big show of accepting high fives and slaps on the back. Watching him, Allison felt a rush of pride. It was a foolish feeling, almost as foolish as the need to rush over to him, throw her arms around his neck and congratulate him with a kiss worthy of one of Collins Jewelers romantic commercials.

It didn't help any that her last memory of Zach—one burned into her heart for all time, she feared—was of him brushing a soft kiss against her lips and leaving her with a murmured, "Dream of me."

Like she'd had any choice! Zach had worked his way under her skin, into her heart, filling her thoughts waking or sleeping, and Allison was afraid she was in big, big trouble.

It took almost fifteen minutes before he made his way over to her, but she felt every step he took toward her. Like standing on a dry beach and waiting for high tide, she anticipated the moment when Zach would overwhelm her, pour over her and pull her deeper into an irresistible undertow…

One good wave, she thought. *That's all it will take.*

"Allison."

His voice sent shivers down her spine, and she fought to the urge to shush him before anyone else could overhear the husky murmur that brought heated kisses to mind. A quick look around reassured her no one else noticed.

So maybe it was only *her* mind.

Trying to focus, she said, "Congratulations. The whole company's thrilled for you."

His lips quirked in a sexy smile. "The whole company's thrilled for free food."

Allison could hardly argue his point. Although everyone had been quick to offer their congratulations, most had been equally as quick to head toward the buffet and bar. "So, tell me, how much are you hating this?"

"You have to ask?"

"I'm so happy to be partly responsible for causing you pain and misery," she teased, "but maybe, just maybe, you can forget about work for one night and enjoy yourself."

Leaning closer, he said, "I wasn't exactly thinking about work last night."

Allison was tempted to ask if he'd enjoyed himself when Daryl stepped to the center of the crowd. "If I could have everyone's attention. Attention, please," he repeated, but with the party atmosphere, no one heard him over the loud music and sounds of celebration.

His eyebrows lifted in challenge, Zach caught Allison's eye, and the day at Bethany's when they'd talked about her life in New York flashed in her memory. Not about to back down, she put her fingers in her mouth and let out a sharp whistle.

A few people close by jumped, a dozen or so heads turned in her direction, and silence fell.

"Thank you, Allison, for that elegant introduction," Daryl said wryly amid laughter from their coworkers. "I wanted to take a moment to congratulate Zach on a job well done. James Collins has a reputation for outstanding workmanship and customer service. It's an honor to be working with his company, and we all have Zach to thank." Lifting the glass he held, Daryl added, "To Zach."

Everyone, Allison included, raised a glass, one she nearly spilled when Zach reached out and caught her wrist before she could take a sip and pulled her to his side. She could feel every eye in the place focused on her, and despite her normal refusal to blend in with the rest of the business crowd, she tried to inconspicuously escape from the hold he had on her arm.

"Zach, what are you doing?" she hissed behind a smile.

Instead of answering her, Zach addressed the entire room once more. "Thank you, Daryl, and thank you all for coming. The Collins account is an exciting opportunity for our entire company, and as usual, I can't wait to get started."

"Oh, great," Brett called out from the back of the crowd. "This was all a trick, wasn't it? You really brought everyone here to work."

Laughter filled the room, and Zach grinned at the good-natured teasing. "Yep. So you better drink up. We've got a planning meeting in five minutes. Actually, I think we can wait until Monday to get back to work. Tonight is for celebrating, but this celebration wouldn't be complete—in fact, it wouldn't even be happening—if not for Allison Warner. Her comments and advice about the presentation were on target. Without her help, I wouldn't be standing here right now, and we wouldn't have much to celebrate. So..." Lifting their still-joined hands, he said, "To Allison."

Stunned, she lifted her eyes to Zach. Meeting his blue eyes, Daryl and the rest of the employees faded away, leaving behind a world where only she and Zach existed. He squeezed her hand, but he might as well have reached inside her chest and squeezed her heart.

If the rest of the room felt as shell-shocked as Allison by Zach's speech, no one let it show. Everyone simply lifted their glasses, ready to finish the toast Daryl had started. "To Allison."

The entire room seemed to shrink as the crowd swelled closer, everyone eager to offer congratulations, but Zach quickly ducked his head before they were separated. "You were right, Allison, and I couldn't have done it without you."

"I didn't—"

"You did," he insisted, giving her hand another squeeze.

She didn't have the chance to reply before the well-wishers intruded. She accepted their congratulations with a smile, quickly downplaying her role, but she could barely focus on what she or anyone else was saying.

She didn't know what shocked her more—Zach taking her advice and using his personal experience to win a client, something he'd sworn he would never do, or his willingness to share the spotlight and give her credit for the idea, something she knew Kevin would never have done.

"Okay, tell me how ya did it!" Beer in hand, Brett Mitchell threw an arm around Allison's shoulders. Young and eager, he was one of the wannabe salesmen Zach so despised, but Allison liked the kid. With his blond hair and wide smile, he had a boy-next-door appeal she figured would make him a great salesman once he had a few more years under his belt.

"How I did what, Brett?" she asked, carefully disengaging from the one-armed hug before she ended up wearing most of his beer.

"How you managed to knock Zach's socks off?"

"Yes, Allison," a humor-filled female voice chimed in. "How *did* you manage that?"

Turning, Allison met Caroline Wilder's gaze. Judging by the older woman's smile, Caroline thought Allison had knocked off more intimate apparel than Zach's socks.

Looking at Zach right then was the last thing Allison

should have done, but her gaze sought him out like a homing beacon. Daryl had already left, but several people still surrounded Zach. He should have been savoring his triumph, basking in the attention. And yet, as if somehow sensing that she watched him, he glanced her way, his eyes locking on hers.

Allison had never considered herself overly susceptible to the power of suggestion, but with Caroline's words as the sounding bell, Allison was seconds away from drooling. All too easily, she could imagine stripping away the tie he'd already loosened. Finishing the job he'd started at the collar by unbuttoning the rest of the buttons on his pale blue dress shirt. Stripping away the leather belt and shoes. Pushing down the slate gray trousers and boxers, Allison decided, leaving nothing but his socks to knock off.

Fortunately, Brett had had enough to drink not to guess the direction of Allison's thoughts and Caroline—well, Caroline was the evil genius who'd implanted those thoughts in the first place, so it was impossible for Allison to keep them secret from her.

Still, Allison maintained, "I lucked out, that's all. I gave Zach some advice, but he's still the one who came up with the proposal and presented it to James Collins."

"Wish I had that kind of luck," Brett said without an ounce of resentment in his voice.

"Just give it time, Brett. Your chance will come."

"Well, right now, it looks like it's my chance to hit the bar."

Shaking her head as Brett made a beeline for the bar, Allison gazed after the young man longer than necessary. Anything to delay facing Caroline Wilder. Finally, though, she had little choice but to turn toward Zach's mother. "This is an amazing party. You did a great job."

"I think you mean *you* did a great job."

"And I think you and your son are both trying to give

me credit where it's not due. I didn't have nearly as much to do with tonight's celebration as either of you are making it sound."

"Zach told me about the advice you gave him for the proposal. Until you came along, my son never made personal connections, but I see how he looks at you and how you look at him."

With the heated glances they'd exchanged, Allison would have had a hard time denying Caroline's claim. But that wasn't about a personal connection so much as it was a physical one. Allison was too realistic to think any relationship with Zach would ever be a lasting one—something that had been far from her mind last night. If he hadn't thrown out a safety net, she would have taken an emotional tumble right into his bed.

Well, *her* bed, technically. And it would have been a mistake.

Her confrontation with Bethany had left Allison feeling like she'd been dragged across hot asphalt for miles. Her emotions were far too raw and vulnerable to build up the tough skin she'd need to guard her heart against Zach. Knowing she was in love with Zach was one thing; Zach finding out she was in love...

"I've never seen him so happy."

"He's just won the contract of his career," Allison said. "Of course he's happy."

"Really, Allison," Caroline said in a chiding rebuke all mothers seemed to have mastered. "I'm sure you've figured out by now business does not make Zach happy."

Needing some time alone, Allison slipped away from the boisterous crowd to find a secluded table on the outside patio. She could still hear the music and laughter coming from inside, but the sounds were muted and the fresh air was free of the scents of fried food and beer.

"I guess it's my turn to find out how angry you are with me."

Allison turned in her chair at the sound of Zach's voice. Her pulse quickened at the sight of him, the faint party lights strung along the patio doing little to dispel the darkness and leaving him cast in mysterious shadow. She tried reminding herself he'd done the right thing in pulling away from her last night, but never before had she wanted something so wrong for her quite so badly...

Swallowing against a throat as dry as the desert, she asked, "Angry?"

He pulled a chair out and inched it closer to hers before taking a seat. "That I spilled the beans and told the entire company how brilliant you are. You know Daryl will offer you a full-time position after this."

Allison waited for a flare of panic, but for the first time the shots didn't fire. The camaraderie of the evening reminded her of the pros of working a long time for one company and a situation where one person's success truly did mean success for all. And she didn't want to worry about the future right then. She wanted to simply enjoy the evening.

"I'm not mad. I'm...touched. It really meant a lot to me, Zach," she added, realizing he couldn't know how much his acknowledgement meant without knowing more of her past. "The other day, you asked me if it was hard to leave New York, my job...Kevin. The truth is, I didn't plan to leave. I came back here for my dad's funeral, but so much had changed."

A burst of laughter spilled out from inside the restaurant, a sharp contrast to her somber memories. "My father was gone, Bethany was barely talking to me. My mother would have been the only reason for me to stay, and she encouraged me to go back. I took a leave of absence, but after a few weeks, I did go back to work. I'd just won the cosmetics contract, and I had another half a dozen ads coming due. I was hoping to lose myself in long hours at the office and literally work my way through my grief."

Zach nodded silently, and Allison had no doubt he knew exactly what she was talking about. "When I got back to work, I found out my winning the cosmetics line was old news. Kevin had pulled in three new clients while I was gone." She could still remember being blindsided by the news when she walked into the office. "I was thrilled for him, but I was also surprised. He had an in with head of the company, and well, most of the time, he acted like it. He took on clients handed over to him by the company's partners, but going after his own accounts wasn't his thing."

Zach shook his head at Allison's description of her ex's work ethic. George Hardaway might have given Zach a recommendation when he first hired on as a kid still in high school, but Zach had known from day one that he'd have to work hard to prove himself. He would have been embarrassed, ashamed even, to ever have the older man think he was coasting along instead of working his ass off.

"Let me guess," he said, "good old Kev was jealous. The accolades you received for winning the cosmetic account inspired him to get off his butt and do some real work?"

Allison gave a mocking laugh, her green eyes glittering in the faint lighting. "Oh, I wish I could say I'd inspired Kevin to work hard, even if showing me up *had* been his motivation. No, I inspired Kevin to steal those ideas...from me."

"He *stole* them?" Sheer incredulity ended up buried by an avalanche of anger for Allison's sake. He bit back a dozen swear words, knowing his negative opinion of her ex wouldn't make Allison feel any better. If anything, that reaction might come off as a criticism against her for falling for a loser.

Allison nodded. "I made it all too easy for him. Back in those days, I worked at home after hours as much as I did at the office. Luckily, I had a laptop that held all my files," she said with a flinch that told him luck had been all on only Kevin's side. "I didn't take it with me when I went home to my father's funeral, and since Kevin and I were living together..."

"It was still stealing," Zach insisted, refusing to let Allison take the blame for trusting the man he assumed she'd loved. "The computer belonged to the company and to you. He had no right to access it, let alone take credit for your campaigns."

No wonder Allison was so afraid to succeed. Not only had her father's death followed her first major professional triumph, so had a personal and professional betrayal—thanks to her jerk of an ex.

"Tell me you called him on it. From what you said about the guy, someone at the top must have realized Kevin couldn't pull his own weight let alone pull in new clients."

"Oh, I tried. First I confronted Kevin who said it was all *my* fault. I was supposed to be there to support him, to encourage him, to be his muse. And yes, he really did use that line, if you can believe it. I wasn't supposed to outshine him, and if I hadn't shown him up the way I had, he wouldn't have *needed* to take my ideas."

This time Zach couldn't hold back his opinion.

Allison nodded at his colorful description. "And that's when I got mad. Up until then, I was too hurt and surprised to be angry. I kept waiting for Kevin to apologize and admit what he did was wrong. When he tried to dump all the blame on me...I went to our boss with my notes and earlier versions of those ads. Proof they were mine. Proof Kevin didn't have. But this was Kevin's old family friend, the one who had personally hired Kevin, brought him to New York, and was grooming him to be one of the big players in the firm. I was only the girlfriend who'd tagged along. Firing Kevin would have reflected badly on him. It would have meant admitting a mistake. Firing me meant nothing."

"Firing you was their loss," Zach argued. "They *deserve* Kevin. They didn't deserve you."

His own words prodded Zach's conscience in way that had him shifting uncomfortably. Allison also deserved better than him. Better than he could offer. He'd thought at first that she was a temporary kind of girl, someone who didn't do serious and might flit from relationship to relationship in the same way she moved from one job to the next.

But he'd seen how important family was to her. Her sorrow when she spoke of her father; her regret over the rift in her relationship with her sister; her excitement over the niece or nephew to come. All of it flashed like warning lights signaling danger ahead. Allison wanted family and forever and everything he couldn't promise. Her bouncing from job to job was nothing more than a safety mechanism to hide her own vulnerability, to keep her from getting hurt... Something that would undoubtedly happen were they to get even more involved.

Disturbed by the thought, he tried getting back on track, saying, "Their loss was my gain. I meant everything I said up there, Allison. I wouldn't have won that contract without you."

Her gaze searched his as she was undoubtedly trying to figure out what had convinced him to take her advice, and he found himself hoping she wouldn't ask, not sure what answer he could give. He'd been working the same way for years, an impassable chasm between his professional and personal life, he still wasn't sure how Allison had bridged that gap and changed his mind. How she'd changed him....

Those warning signs loomed ever larger on the horizon. *Last Chance. Turn Back Now. No Exit Ahead.*

Almost as if sensing his rising panic, Allison said, "Then I guess it's time for both of us to celebrate, and I know there are still people around who want to congratulate you."

"Like the kid?"

"What kid?"

"The one who was hanging all over you when you were talking to my mom."

"You mean Brett? He's—" Her eyes widened and her dimple flashed as she teased, "Don't tell me you're jealous, Zach Wilder."

"Naw," he said, denying the possibility and the possessive surge he'd felt when the younger man had pulled Allison into a one-armed hug. "He's not your type."

"I have a type?"

"Sure. First of all, he's just a kid. Way too much of a pushover for you and not nearly enough of a challenge."

"Who says I like challenging men?"

"I do. You challenge me all the time."

One corner of her mouth kicked up in appreciation of his play on words. "Brett's the newest sales assistant. He started at Knox right before I did." At Zach's groan, she added, "I know what you're thinking, but you might end up liking him."

"Yeah, why is that?"

"Well, he's pretty much your biggest fan, and there's something about him that reminds me of you. Come on. I'll introduce you," she said, rising to her feet.

"Allie—"

"Come on," she insisted, proving his point about bossing men around as she ignored his protest, grabbed his arm and led the way back inside and over to Brett.

He did look hungry, Zach thought as the two of them talked shop for a few minutes, but also earnest and eager to please. And Allison didn't know what she was talking about comparing the two of them. He'd never been like this happy-go-lucky puppy of a kid.

Yeah, okay, when George Hardaway installed the alarm in his mother's house a dozen years ago, Zach had asked one or two or…twenty questions about the system, the installation, the tools the man used. And he might have called the guy a few times to remind him of his promise to get Zach a job as an apprentice that first summer. And maybe…Allison was right. Maybe he had been like this kid a long, long time ago.

And maybe he owed it to George to return the favor the older man had done for him. But it wasn't George he was thinking of as he offered to take Brett along on his next walk-through of a condo project he'd been working on. It was Allison and the pleasure he took in making her smile.

Chapter Eleven

"This is it," Zach said, and Allison turned her car on to a brick half-circle driveway.

When Caroline asked Allison to drive Zach home, just to be safe after the few beers he'd had to drink, she'd hesitated for a brief moment. She'd only had one beer along with enough greasy bar food to coat her stomach and hips for weeks to come, so she was certainly capable of fulfilling designated driver duties. It wasn't the drive part that worried her, but the home part. As in Zach's home. The two of them alone at Zach's home.

Last night, dangerous emotional land mines had kept them from crossing uncharted territory. But what would stop them tonight?

What should stop them? If she went in with both eyes open and focused on the upcoming promotion that would have Zach living in airports and hotels, he'd never have to know she'd so foolishly fallen for him. And she could have tonight. This moment. Right here, right now.

Indecision still plaguing her, Allison focused on the house. "This isn't what I expected." Nestled amid desert landscaping on a large lot, the Spanish-style house with its flat roof and arched entryway had a classic, old-world feel. An intricate bronze-colored wrought iron gate opened into the patio braced by aged wooden beams. "It's so…"

"So what?" he prodded when her voice trailed away.

Allison waited until she'd climbed from the car and met Zach at the front grill before she explained, "So…*not you.*"

He chuckled. "And what would be me?"

"I don't know. I guess I pictured a place like Knox."

"You thought I'd live in an office building? I'm dedicated but not that dedicated," he told her with a sideways glance as their footsteps tapped on the stones and motion-activated sensors lighted the way like magic. Cactus, lantana and sage lined the path, and a rustle off to the left alerted Allison to other desert survivors who still called this area northwest of Phoenix home—lizards, ground squirrels, rabbits, coyotes, and even javelina though she hadn't seen one in years.

"No, not an office building, but a place filled with glass and granite and steel…not this."

"Disappointed?"

"Are you kidding? This place is great," she said, captivated by the house's rustic desert charm.

The gate squeaked slightly as Zach pushed it open, and with a grin he admitted, "Keep forgetting to fix that."

"Oh, I don't know. That's one of those touches that makes a house feel like home."

He laughed. "That's an excuse for poor home maintenance I've never used before."

"It's not poor maintenance," Allison argued. "It's reassurance. In the house where I grew up, there was a squeaky step near the landing my dad never fixed. Once he heard that squeak, he knew Bethany and I were home safe, and he could go to sleep."

"Couldn't you have skipped over the squeaky step so he wouldn't have known what time you got in?"

"And cause my dad a sleepless night? Nah, we wouldn't have done that."

In the faint light of the porch, Zach turned to lead her across the patio with its colorful Mexican tile to the oversized front door but not before she caught the look in his eyes. A loneliness and longing that tugged at her heart. Feeling her way as carefully as she would navigating the spiny cactus in his front yard, she said, "I'm sure your mother worried about you on nights you stayed out late."

"We looked out for each other, but my mother worked two jobs most of the time I was a teenager. She counted on me to take care of myself."

Once Zach disabled the alarm and hit the lights, Allison had a faint impression of warm beige walls, wood floors, and oversized leather furniture. The effect was rustic and masculine, suiting the house and the man who lived there. She wasn't sure exactly when they stopped talking, but she was well aware of all they weren't saying when Zach stepped closer.

She felt a little stalked, one of those rabbits faced with a coyote's stealthy approach. Indecisive, spellbound, unsure which direction to flee...

"So this is it. We did it. We survived two weeks working together."

But Allison was no helpless bunny, and she didn't want to run. "Thanks to you, that was a far greater challenge than winning the account."

"Thanks to me?"

"You are notoriously difficult."

Zach laughed. "The worst part is going to be facing Daryl and having to admit that he was right."

"We did make a good team," she admitted. *"Eventually."*

Meeting his gaze, the teasing moment faded away along with the last of Allison's reservations. He might have spent most of his life taking care of himself, and one night couldn't change that, but she wanted this one night to show how much she cared. Hoping she wasn't making a huge mistake, she had to point out, "We do still work together."

But instead of agreeing with her, instead of taking a step back, Zach murmured, "Not until Monday."

And Monday, like work, suddenly seemed far, far away, especially when Zach and his bedroom were much, much closer.

Reading her answer in her eyes, he pulled her into his arms and claimed her with a kiss so hot the air seemed to sizzle around them. It stole her breath and left her gasping for more. Rising on her toes, she pressed her body to his. Close, then closer until she could hear his ragged breathing and feel his heart thundering. Until she resented every article of clothing, every millimeter of distance separating them.

He muttered her name against her mouth, her cheek, her throat. Each husky whisper and arousing touch sent shivers running up and down her spine. She thought she just might melt into the floor, but Zach pulled her tight, and she melted into him instead.

Allison fumbled with the buttons on his shirt, but their small size and tight fit resisted her clumsy efforts, so she pulled the tails from his trousers instead. Beneath the crisp material, each brush of her palms over the smooth skin of his back and tight muscles of his stomach made her greedy for more.

"Make love to me, Zach."

He groaned her name in what she might have thought was

a protest until he swept her up into his arms. Allison smothered her startled laughter against his neck, breathing in the scent of his skin and the anticipation of what was to come as he carried her into the bedroom. Zach didn't turn on the lamp but between the moon streaming through the open curtains and the light from the hallway, the bed was awash in a soft glow.

She could see the intensity in his dark eyes as he laid her on the bed and stripped off his shirt. When he sank down next to her, she had the freedom to explore his broad shoulders, muscled chest and stomach, first with her eyes and then with her hands. His hair-roughened skin tickled her palms, but it was Zach who sucked in a quick breath when her fingertips brushed his abdomen as she worked the buckle on his belt.

"This was an amazing day for you," she whispered.

"Tonight's turning out to be even more amazing," he vowed, his deep voice rough with desire, but Allison knew better than to take words murmured against heated skin to heart. She *knew* better.

Still, she had to take in a deep breath before she added, "Winning the Collins account—"

The hunger in his gaze turned slightly incredulous as he pulled back to meet her gaze. "You might not believe this, Allie, but I really don't want to talk about work right now."

"So I don't have to worry then? That I'm taking advantage of your emotional state?"

He gave a bark of laughter as he caught her body to his and rolled her beneath him. "You've had the advantage since we met. Each time I look at you, all I can think of is doing this…and this…and this…"

Allison barely noticed as Zach stripped away her clothes, except when it meant she had to stop kissing him to toss aside her shirt or shimmy out of her skirt. His fingertips trailed down her throat to the curve of her breast. Her nipple tightened in anticipation, and her whole body arched to his touch. Need poured through her, melting muscle and bone until her body felt liquefied, bound to Zach's magnetic pull as completely as the oceans were to the moon. She rose and fell with every stroke—along her breasts, her belly, her thighs...

There was something special about their lovemaking, something rare and precious and...finite. But Allison didn't want to think about the future when the present held such promise. His body sank into hers, and she welcomed him just as she'd welcomed his kiss, his touch. Her arms and legs wrapped tight, never wanting to let him go...

Slowly, he began to move, a gradually increasing pace destined to drive her wild. Her body rose and fell with every thrust, again and again until golden sunbursts flared behind her eyelids and the pleasure broke over them in a glorious shower that sent them drifting softly back to earth, to the comfort of each other's arms.

Zach awoke Monday morning, and for the first time in memory, he didn't want to go to work. Of course, for the first time in memory, he also had a beautiful woman sleeping in his bed. He'd had affairs before, but rarely had a woman spent the night and *never* the entire weekend. But after their first time making love, he hadn't wanted to let Allison go. They'd spent the weekend locked in the world of make-believe where Monday would never come.

But the game of pretend couldn't last forever, and reality was seeing each other at work in less than two hours.

Seated on the bed beside a still sleeping Allison, Zach reached out to brush her hair back from her forehead. The morning sunlight cutting through the blinds turned her hair to gold. She was wearing one of his dress shirts, one he'd never wear again without thinking of her, but he already knew every inch of skin hidden beneath the material. Knew it, and yet ached to explore every one of her curves all over again. She amazed him. She was bold and confident, but at the same time caring and vulnerable. And the last thing he wanted to do was hurt her...

As if sensing the weight of his gaze, her eyes fluttered open. She pushed her hair back from her eyes and yet not a hint of sleep clouded her expression. When she spoke, it was like she'd picked up on the conversation he'd been having in his own mind. "So this is it. Back to work." Allison smiled, but the expression looked a little forced and vulnerability shook the edges of her smile.

She was making this easy on him, saying all the things he didn't want to say so he wouldn't have to feel guilty. Which only made him feel like even more of an SOB. "Allie—"

"It's okay, Zach. Really." She climbed from the bed and started collecting the clothes he'd scattered throughout the bedroom again and again, barely able to be in the same room with her without stripping them off. "I know you're probably worried that I'll—I don't know. Be so overwhelmed with lust that I'll grab you in the middle of a meeting for a make out session, but I promise to restrain myself."

"Too bad."

"Yeah, isn't it?" Her smile fell away completely, stripping away Allison's tough façade and leaving only the vulnerable woman behind.

He knew the right decision would be to end things now. To chalk their amazing time together up to a single weekend of passion and let them both get back to their lives. Winning the Collins contract was only the tip of the iceberg when it came to the work ahead of him, and the decision about VP was supposed to be announced in the next week. A promotion that meant almost constant traveling, a challenge to even the strongest relationships, forget one just starting out.

And wouldn't it be better to let go now before that new-ness wore off?

Let her go...let her go...let her go... Think of the promo-tion, think of San Francisco, think of moving up and moving on.

The motto that had always inspired him in the past fell short. And—another first—he couldn't do it. Faced with a choice between his personal life and his career, and he couldn't make the right one.

"I don't want to stop seeing you, Allie." Her green eyes widened as she took a shaky step backward, her shirt tangled in her hands, and Zach wondered if he wasn't about to make an enormous fool of himself. Maybe he wanted their relation-ship to continue, but was he so certain Allison wanted the same? Swallowing hard, he took a step forward, erasing the distance she'd put between them and then some.

"I know it probably sounds crazy. I can't pretend it doesn't, and—hell, I don't even know what I'm offering. You pointed out more than once that I'd make a terrible boyfriend. I'm going to be swamped with this new account and the promo-tion to VP means I'll be traveling all the time..."

His voice trailed off. "You deserve so much better."

So much more than he had to offer.

With the promotion only days away, a few stolen moments over the next week or so would be all they would have. And for Allison, Zach knew it would never be enough. Preparing himself for her rejection, he stepped back from the bed as if those few feet could somehow distance him from the loss to come.

Clearing her throat, Allison said, "Well, when you put it all like that, how could I possibly refuse?"

Relief washed over him, a wave damn near strong enough to knock him off his feet. This mattered; *Allison* mattered, more than he wanted to admit. More than...

The thought hovered on the edges of his subconscious, but he pushed it aside as he rescued the twisted shirt from her hands, once again tossing her clothes aside, this time without even having to take them off. He pulled back a mere inch from kissing her with a mock frown. "There still can't be any make out sessions in the conference room."

Allison's laughter gave voice to all the crazy, wild happiness he felt inside. "Then I guess I'll just have to have my way with you now."

Chapter Twelve

Zach walked into work, fighting the urge to whistle. He couldn't remember the last time he'd felt so relaxed, so at ease. But why shouldn't he? Everything was falling in place for him. He and Allison had spent every free moment together since the party last Friday. Seeing her at work wasn't as difficult as he thought it might be. For all her teasing, Allison had treated him the same as she had the week before, before they'd slept together.

If anyone was having a hard time keeping his hands to himself, Zach admitted ruefully, it was him.

Fortunately and as he'd predicted, the work she'd done on the Collins proposal had gotten her noticed. Daryl had asked her to help out another salesman when she wasn't working with Zach. To his surprise, she hadn't talked about leaving Knox again or about her plan to move on to yet another temp job. And the more he thought about it, the more he realized Allison *should* stay at Knox.

She'd done an amazing job; Daryl and the rest of the sales staff liked her. Hell, she was even on Martha's good side—a place Zach rarely managed to venture. She should stay—especially since in a few weeks Zach would be out of the office more than he'd be around. The board would be coming back any day now with a decision for the VP position, and Zach knew he was in. After winning the Collins account, not to mention all the work he'd done in the past six years, how could they not give him the promotion?

"You're late again." Martha's voice cut into his thoughts as he walked by the reception desk.

Zach's eyebrows rose. "Late? It's not even eight o'clock."

"Exactly," she announced with a hint of spark in her normally serious expression. "When do you ever get here after me? Other than this past week?"

Zach frowned. He had been taking his time coming in to the office, unwilling to leave Allison in the morning. And not just reluctant to leave her bed, although that was certainly part of it. That morning, they'd lingered over coffee on her back patio, enjoying the cool morning and arguing over which section of the paper he got to read first. She'd held the business section out of reach, telling him he needed to focus on the "Life" section a bit more.

"I didn't have any appointments first thing. If I had—"

"Zach, I'm teasing," Martha interrupted. "You deserve some time to yourself. Everyone knows how hard you work around here."

Rolling his shoulders, he tried to dislodge the sudden uncertainty pressing down on him. He did deserve some time—even if he wasn't exactly spending that time to himself. Coming in *on time* instead of an hour and a half early certainly didn't mean he was losing his edge.

He was still trying to convince himself later that morning when Daryl asked him to come into his office. He should have expected what was to come, but his boss's announcement that the board had come to a decision caught him off guard. Somehow he thought they'd contact him directly rather than going through Daryl and a conference call. Sinking into the leather chair across from Daryl's desk, he greeted the board members across the intercom and listened as they told him how close of a decision it had been as they'd compared the candidates and weighed who would be best for the job before making their choice.

Zach wasn't exactly sure when the news sunk in that what he was hearing wasn't congratulations, but condolences.

"So, you see, Zach," the faceless, impersonal voice crackled over the speaker, "although your track record is impressive, we feel a more experienced salesman would be better suited for the vice president position."

The compliments and consolation droned on, but Zach stopped listening after the initial rejection. Pretty it up as much as you want, no still meant no. And he'd been so damn sure the answer would be yes! The loss broadsided him, knocking him off center and leaving him listing and rudderless. Out of control.

Was this how it felt, he wondered dimly, when his father found out Caroline was pregnant? When Nathan Wilder had watched all his dreams slip out of his grasp, knowing there wasn't a damn thing he could do about it?

He kept his expression carefully blank. The owner of the disembodied voice couldn't see him, but Daryl sat across the gleaming cherry desk, watching closely.

When the meaningless buzz of meaningless words coming from the speakerphone finally ceased, Zach replied without a hint of what he really thought revealed in his voice. "Thank you for considering me. I'm sure you made the right choice."

Daryl was silent as he disconnected the call, as if waiting for Zach's outburst. "I'm sorry, Zach."

Shoving out of the leather armchair, Zach braced his palms on the desk. "Dammit, Daryl, Bob Henderson hasn't brought in one new account since I started working sales!"

"But the accounts he has—"

"Are some of the biggest in California," Zach finished for his boss. "Sitting on the same damn accounts for six years does not mean that Bob is a good salesman. It means he *was* a good salesman."

Daryl stood and circled his desk. "No one is questioning the success you've had since you joined the sales team. You should be proud."

Zach supposed that was how he *should* feel. Instead the bitter taste of rejection remained.

"Think of it this way. You get to stay on top of the Collins project. I know it would have killed you to pass that job off to another salesman. Your turn will come, Zach, and even though I know you're disappointed, I'm glad you are still part of our team."

Zach knew he was expected to toe the company line and agree with Daryl's pep talk, but he couldn't do it. After spending the past weeks talking himself up, literally selling himself for the sake of the promotion, he'd run out of things to say. The man with the silver tongue, the salesperson who could sell the proverbial icemaker to an Eskimo, had failed. He hadn't been able to make the most important sale. He couldn't get the corporate office to buy into him as the VP of sales.

Instead, he gave an abrupt nod and left his boss's office. The plush burgundy carpet leading the way to his door was the same as the day before, but Zach felt as though he were slugging through knee-high marshland.

He could feel himself being dragged down, his sky-high goals drifting further and further out of reach, and he knew he had to break free before it was too late. Maybe the VP position was only one missed promotion, but before long, it would be one lost bid, one dropped client, then another and another.

How many times had he reminded himself he couldn't have a personal life and expect to get ahead in business? He'd known that for years yet he'd let himself be distracted, and now he was paying.

He rounded the corner to his office and almost ran into Allison. She stopped short and braced her hands on his chest. Her familiar touch burned into him, and he jerked back but not before he felt like he wore her brand on his skin.

"Good morning." Her smile was as bright as ever, the dimple in her right cheek flashing, but for Zach, it was like he'd come out of a subterranean cave and everything bright and beautiful could only cause him pain.

"I can't talk right now, Allison."

The loss of the promotion hit harder than he would have expected, and the anger and frustration he'd buried during the conference call were rising to the surface—smoldering, virulent, and ready to explode.

"What's wrong?" she asked as she reversed direction and dogged his heels when the best thing for both of them would be for her to leave him alone. "You might as well tell me. You know how persistent I am."

He knew. And if Allison wanted to know what was wrong… Zach waited until they reached his office and he'd closed the door to say, "Bob Henderson got the promotion."

"Oh, Zach, I'm so sorry." She exhaled a sigh, her earlier cheer deserting her. But while Zach could see for himself that Allison *was* sorry, completely missing from her expression was any sign of surprise. Any at all.

"I should have had that promotion," he argued. "I should have—"

"Should have what? Worked harder, longer? Put in twenty hour days instead of your usual fourteen?"

He snorted. "Sure as hell isn't what Bob Henderson did."

"No, it's not. But he still got the promotion. Do you know why?"

Zach didn't give a damn why Bob got the promotion. He couldn't see beyond the reason why *he* hadn't. "It doesn't matter. It's too late now."

Persistent as promised, Allison refused to let go. "The VP job is a supervisory position. One that's perfect for him. But it isn't the job for you."

Not the job for him, Zach thought grimly. *The board of directors couldn't have said it better.*

"Allison—just forget it."

"You're a great salesman, Zach. Look at the job you did with James Collins."

"I have other contacts," he ground out from jaws nearly locked together, "other bids in the works. I should have been going after those instead of—" He cut off again, but it was too late.

Allison took a step back, her face turning pale. "You think you lost the promotion because of our—" She cut off her own words, stopping short of identifying what they'd shared as a relationship. "You think you lost the promotion because of *me*?"

"I knew this wouldn't work, Allison. I'm sorry."

Color rushed back into her cheeks, and her green eyes snapped with anger. "I'm sorry, too, Zach. In fact, I feel sorry for you. Success isn't about how many promotions you can chalk up before you're thirty. Success is enjoying what you do. If you'd stop to think about something other than moving up the ladder, you might even realize how much you'd hate working in a management position!"

"You're one to talk, aren't you? You already have a job you hate, not to mention a dozen or so hobbies you're no good at. Tell me, Allison, how happy are you?"

The sudden buzz of the intercom jarred them apart like boxers to their corners at the ring of the bell. Martha's voice sounded over the speaker. "Zach, Mr. Collins is on line one."

Taking a deep breath to try to calm the volatile emotions rippling through the room like aftershocks from a quake, he said, "I can't do this. Not here, not now."

Allison met his gaze, her green eyes unflinching. "There won't be a later," she warned softly.

He'd known. He'd known from the start that one day he would have to make a choice. Turning his back on Allison, he reached for the phone.

Zach didn't bother to glance away from his computer when he heard the knock. "Come in," he barked.

He heard the door open, but when the intruder didn't speak, Zach kept working. It was the only thing to keep him going since the failed promotion.

It's not the promotion, a know-it-all voice goaded. Dismal failure haunted him with wounded green eyes every time he closed his eyes, but Zach had found a cure. The same prescription he'd followed for years. He kept working.

"Zach…" Daryl's voice buzzed on the edge of his thoughts, barely rising above the constant electronic hum of the hard drive.

Without looking away from the schematics for a new shopping mall in the northwest valley, Zach said, "Did you see the file I emailed you? The contract's not as big as the Collins account, but it's a decent-sized job."

"I saw it, but that's not what I want to talk to you about."

Something in his boss's voice caught his attention, and Zach pulled his gaze away from the computer screen that had become his window to the rest of the world for the past week. He had to blink a few times to retrain his eyes to focus on something other than flat-screen pixels.

He'd barely seen Allison since their argument. He didn't know how she'd convinced Daryl, but lately she'd been working with the other salesmen. He kept expecting the day to come when she was no longer at Knox, when she would move on to another temp job. But every now and then, he'd hear her laughter or sense the change in the air when she walked by his office. Each time, he had to lock his muscles into place, sometimes going as far as to grab hold of the arms of his chair to keep from running after her.

He owed her an apology; he'd acted like a total ass, turning his temper loose on her when he had only himself to blame.

A worried frown pulled at Daryl's eyebrows, and Zach immediately demanded, "What's wrong?" Had something happened to Allison? Grim possibilities ran through his mind—accidents, illness, injuries…

"It's Bob Henderson."

"What?" His rival was the last person who would have come to mind, and Zach blankly asked, "What about him?"

"He had a heart attack at work yesterday. From what I understand, he's stabilized, but the cardiologist has recommended bypass surgery. With the recovery time required, it's unlikely he'll be back to work any time soon, and if he does return, it will be on a part-time basis. He's stepping down from the VP position."

Zach knew where his boss was going with the conversation, but after the disappointment of losing the promotion, he couldn't believe what he was hearing.

Daryl seemed to have sensed as much because he added, "You have an interview in San Francisco tomorrow, but it's little more than a formality. The job's yours."

His boss waited expectantly, but Zach still couldn't get beyond a feeling of disbelief. "What about all the reasons I wasn't right for the job? Did the extra week of experience make that big of a difference?"

"It was a close call between you and Bob to begin with, and I have no doubt you'll prove any detractors wrong in no time. That is...if you still want the job."

If he still wanted the job... Of course he wanted the job. Didn't he?

Allison's laughing face flashed through his thoughts, and for a moment, Zach considered what life might be like if he stayed. If they made up from the fight they'd had, if they gave a relationship a shot. He knew Allison wanted to get married and have a family. Like a DVD on fast-forward, his thoughts rushed ahead to Allison holding a blond-haired, green-eyed girl or maybe a dark-haired boy.

But then the DVD playing in his mind skipped backward, to his father's darkened den where his old man spent countless hours watching the glory days of his high school football career, filled with bitterness over the life he could have had...

"I still want it," Zach told Daryl, almost grimly.

The older man studied Zach silently, almost as if trying to read into his thoughts. "I want you to know, you had my support the first time around. I had my doubts when you first applied for the position, but your work with Allison changed my mind."

"What does Allison have to do with anything?"

Behind his wire-rimmed glasses, Daryl's speculative gaze had Zach wondering if his relationship with Allison wasn't such a secret after all. "The first time I met Allison, I knew there was something special about her."

Zach had known it as well. Known it and fought it with every cell in his body, but that was hardly something he wanted to discuss with his boss. "Daryl—"

"Untapped potential. I saw it right away, and you were the one who brought out the best in her. That's what a manager needs to do. I wasn't sure you had it in you, but you proved me wrong, Zach."

"Allie never needed me to bring out the best in her," Zach protested quietly. "She's amazing all on her own."

But being with Allison had done what Zach always feared a relationship would. It had brought out the *worst* in him. The part of himself he'd long sought to ignore, to deny. The part of him that was every bit his father's son. *Coulda had it all if it wasn't for you...*

How many times had Zach faced his father's accusations only to throw those same words back at Allison? He'd blamed her for losing the promotion when, in truth, he wouldn't have been in the running if not for her.

Regret clutched his gut, and Zach knew. He couldn't do to Allison what his father had done to his mother and him.

Looking at Daryl, he asked, "When's my flight?"

Allison thought maybe if she stayed angry, the pain would start to ease before her anger faded away. So she spent her mornings blow drying her hair, putting on her makeup and driving into work replaying every minute of her argument with Zach.

She'd hated seeing him beat himself up over a decision he had no control over. No one could have done more for that promotion. Over the past three weeks, she'd witnessed how hard he worked, and she'd wanted Zach to be as proud of himself as she was of him—promotion or no promotion.

She'd tried to convince him of that until it hit her like a slap in the face. The frustration and regret pulsing beneath the surface wasn't because Zach blamed himself—he blamed her. She loved him, and yet Zach saw their relationship as nothing more than a convenient excuse for his failure—just like Kevin had.

And she only had herself to blame. How many times had

Zach warned her that business came first? Did she really think she was so special or the time they spent together so spectacular that he would suddenly change his mind, giving up goals he'd spent a lifetime climbing?

Yes, Allison admitted as she closed her car door with more force than necessary. That was exactly what she'd hoped, which only went to prove she was a bigger fool than she might have thought.

Fortunately, she hadn't had to see her foolishness reflected back to her in Zach's blue eyes. She'd barely seen him since their fight. One of the newest sales assistants had quit without notice and Allison was doing her best to help the overloaded staff. Daryl had made it clear she had a job at Knox for as long as she wanted, but Allison had agreed to stay only until they found a replacement.

Remember Plan A...

As Allison waited for the elevator to take her to the fourth floor, she could almost laugh at her earlier certainty that another few weeks working with Zach wouldn't have any effect on the goals *she'd* made. She couldn't imagine a backup plan that could have saved her from her mistake in falling in love with Zach Wilder.

She'd barely stepped off the elevator when Brett came jogging toward her. "Hey, Allison, did you hear the news?"

"Hear what?" she asked when he fell in step beside her. "No. Let me guess."

She didn't think the kid could manage a conversation without bringing up Zach's name. His admiration had blown into a major case of hero worship, but that was Allison's fault, too. She'd been the one to encourage Zach to work with the sales assistant. She was still a little surprised he'd taken on the task.

"Zach won yet another major account," Allison guessed.

"No. He got the promotion."

She met Brett's excited gaze with a blank one of her own. "What promotion? I didn't hear he was up for another promotion."

"Not another promotion. The VP job." His excitement mellowed slightly as he explained, "Bob Henderson suffered a heart attack the other day. He's gonna be okay, but he isn't taking the promotion. Zach's got an interview today, but everyone knows he's got a lock on the job."

"So, he's—" Allison's steps slowed "—he's already left for California?"

"Yeah. He'll be there for a week, checking things out. And he's asked me to keep an eye on his accounts while he's gone. Can you believe it? I mean, I guess they won't be his accounts for much longer, but he still left me in charge. Pretty cool, huh?"

"All of his accounts?" Thinking of Riana Collins and her skintight suits, Allison winced. The woman would eat Brett alive and still have room for dessert.

He laughed. "Zach warned me about Riana Collins. I've got it all under control."

"Uh-huh."

The young man grinned, clearly anticipating life as a tasty morsel. "And Zach wanted me to find out when a good time was for me to stop by your place."

"My place?"

"Yeah, to set up your alarm. He told me he didn't have a chance to do it before he left." Brett rolled his eyes. "He insisted I handle the install. Said it would build character. So when— Hey, are you okay?"

Forcing a smile, she said, "Sure, I'm fine."

"You thought he forgot, didn't you?"

"He's kind of had a lot on his mind lately." So much that he'd left without finding the time to tell her goodbye…

"He didn't forget," Brett reassured her. "I almost think he

was more worried about getting your alarm installed than he was about me taking over his accounts, if you can believe it."

As a matter of fact, she couldn't. No doubt the alarm system was some kind of a parting gift—the Zach Wilder version of breakup jewelry. She couldn't let herself believe it might mean something more—that Zach cared about her or was worried about leaving her. "We'll set something up next week if *you're* not too busy with all this new responsibility. I'm really proud of you, Brett."

"Ah, it's no big deal." Embarrassed, he shrugged off her praise. "Zach's the one you should really be proud of. I heard he'll be one of the company's youngest VPs. Think I'll have what it takes to make VP someday?"

The eager gleam lighting Brett's face made Allison smile despite her mood. "Of course you will. You can do anything you put your mind to."

"Thanks, Allison! I'll catch you later."

Her smile faded as Brett disappeared down the hall. She walked slowly toward the empty office she'd been using and sank down behind the desk.

You can do anything...

Her own words echoed in her thoughts, weighing her down until she didn't think she'd be able to move from her chair. That certainly wasn't what she'd said to Zach. She hadn't encouraged him at all.

Why? Why had she been so sure he would hate the VP job?

Because he was such a good salesman she couldn't see him in a different role? Because she worried that no promotion, no step up the ladder no matter how high, would truly make him happy?

Or were her reasons more personal than that? Deep down, had she wanted Bob Henderson to receive the promotion so Zach would stay in Phoenix?

An undeniable truth resounded in that thought. She'd tried to hold Zach back, the same way he always feared being in a relationship would.

She should have supported him. She should have encouraged him to go after his dreams even if had meant leaving her behind. At least then, maybe she would have had the chance to say goodbye.

Chapter Thirteen

Zach stepped through the airport's automatic doors and immediately felt the dip in temperature from the sunny, ninety-degree weather he'd come from to the cool, damp air of San Francisco. A dull haze blocked the sun, giving the sky a pre-dawn feel even though it was almost noon. As Zach flagged down a cab, he reminded himself he wasn't there for the weather. He was there for the job, for the promotion he'd counted on.

And one he'd received by default.

Knox Security chose their man for the job, and it hadn't been Zach.

Was that why the feeling of excitement was missing? Because he hadn't actually earned the promotion?

He shoved the thought aside. Like a second string quarterback called into the game for the injured star, Zach might not be the coach's first choice, but he'd earn the right to keep playing.

He frowned; sports analogies weren't his thing. His dad

was always the one who quoted stats, records and sports cli-chés. But the story did parallel Zach's situation. This was his chance, and it was up to him to make the most of it.

His determination lasted through flagging down a cab, throwing his overnight bag in the backseat and climbing into the vehicle, but when the driver asked where he wanted to go, the name of the hotel froze in his throat. He should go to the room and prepare for his morning meeting, but before he even knew what he was going to say, he heard the words, "San Francisco General."

He almost changed his mind a half a dozen times during the ride, but before long, he was walking through the sterile, antiseptic-smelling corridors toward Bob Henderson's room. Pushing the door open, Zach could see only one bed was oc-cupied. A silver-haired man whose pale skin was nearly as white as the sheets lay in the far bed, hooked up to medicine and machines by tubes and wires. Judging by his deep breath-ing, the man was asleep.

Tightening his grip on the strap of the overnight bag he'd slung over his shoulder, Zach took a step back, ready to leave the man in peace.

A weak voice stopped him in his tracks. "Look who's here. Zach Wilder."

Red-rimmed eyes stared at him from the bed, and Zach stepped forward. "I don't think we've ever met."

"Never have. But I recognize you from your picture in the company newsletter. Salesman of the year five years run-ning."

A hint of sarcasm underscored the words, but Zach didn't blame the other man. To succeed at winning that goal only to lose it in a matter of days would leave anyone bitter.

"So, they brought you in to take my place."

"Yeah," Zach said, feeling guilty even though none of this was his fault. He pulled a hardback novel from the outside pocket of his overnight bag. "I picked this up for you." The spy novel had hit the bestsellers' list a few weeks ago. "It's supposed to be good."

"Thanks. Guess I'll have plenty of time for reading now."

Zach set the book on a small shelf by the bed. A huge bouquet took up most of the space. "Nice flowers."

"Nothing but the best from Knox."

"They're from the company?" Zach asked as he touched a peach rose petal. The silky-soft texture and pale color reminded him of Allison's skin. The floral scent teased his senses—almost like she stood beside him—and he reluctantly pulled his hand away.

He looked around the room, expecting to see more flowers, balloons or cards from friends and family, but the room was conspicuously bare. The absence of any personal concern or well wishes struck Zach as sad. It also struck a little too close to home.

He didn't know anything about Henderson's life outside of work. Was he married? Did he have kids, grandkids? Any family at all?

For a few short weeks, Zach had had Allison. He'd had her smiles, her laughter, her passion… He'd also had her care and concern as she scolded him for working too hard and not getting enough sleep. They were comments he normally would have brushed off, confident he knew best when it came to what he needed to be happy. The truth was, until Allison, he simply hadn't known what he was missing.

"I spent my career waiting for this moment."

Zach could have been the one speaking the words. Bob stared at the ceiling as he added, "I was pretty hot stuff myself before you came along. Won some big clients no one else could even talk to. Worked hard at bringing in the latest systems when technology started changing so fast."

Those accomplishments had happened well over a decade

ago, but Zach wasn't going to point that out. "You've done a lot to be proud of."

"Yeah," the older man agreed, his response sounding as hollow as Zach's compliment. "I worked a lotta years, waiting for this promotion."

"You know you're the one they wanted," Zach pointed out, unable to shake the feeling that something wasn't right. He should have been happier than this, ready to grab hold of the promotion and not let go, no matter how it had fallen into his hands.

But he couldn't stop himself from adding, "Knox will hold the VP position open for you if you ask. Take a leave of absence, and I bet in a few months, you'll be back and ready to take over."

Bob shook his head. "If the past few days have taught me anything, it's that I'm not the man for the job. Not anymore. After this, I don't think I'm up for the extra hours and extra stress involved in running the department."

He heaved a sigh, sinking further back onto his pillows. "You're lucky, kid, to be moving up as fast as you are. You're young enough to climb the corporate ladder all the way to CEO and still have time to enjoy the view from the top."

Moving up and moving on. The motto had marked his every career change. Always reaching for something better. But it wasn't Bob's prediction that echoed in his thoughts as he wished the man well and left the hospital. Instead, another phrase entirely kept ringing in his ears.

Enjoy the view from the top...

Would he reach those heights in the next ten, fifteen years? And if he did, would he have someone to celebrate with him? Or would the occasion be marked only with a bouquet from the company or another gold watch?

* * *

Zach rubbed his eyes, feeling the strain of staring at the screen for so many hours. He supposed he should have been used to it by now but—

"Zach? Honey, what are you doing here?"

His mother's voice sounded behind him in the pre-dawn darkness. The flickering light from the television offered the only illumination as he shifted in the recliner and glanced over his shoulder. Caroline stood in the doorway wearing a belted silk robe he'd bought her for Christmas a few years ago. "Sorry, Mom. I didn't mean to wake you."

"That's okay. But why aren't you still in San Francisco? I thought you were staying through until Monday."

"I caught a late flight back."

His mother hesitated before she said, "Did the meetings not go well?"

"Went great. The job's mine."

"Well, that's wonderful." Her enthusiasm sounded forced, but her confusion was all too real as she asked, "But what are you doing here watching those old videos?"

Unsure how to explain why he'd shown up at her house in the middle of the night, he turned back to the grainy amateur video. The home team, wearing red jerseys and white pants, were on offense. The quarterback took a five-step drop, set his feet, and threw a ten-yard pass. The wide receiver leapt, seeming to defy gravity with a one-handed catch, and sprinted down the field, evading blue and gray defenders, to score a touchdown.

Zach watched the quarterback—his father—race down the field to greet his teammate in the end zone, arms raised high in victory. He couldn't begin to imagine how many hours his father had sat in the darkened den, drinking scotch, watching the old videos and talking about the "good ole days." Zach hadn't seen the tapes in years.

Back when he was still a kid, he'd watched with the hope of pleasing his old man, of finding some way to gain his father's approval. By the time he was a teenager, though, they'd butted heads so many times over so many things that Zach pretty much refused to set foot in his father's haven or to watch the games again.

Now, he wished he had. Now, as an adult, he saw all the details he'd missed as a child. "He wasn't that good," he said softly.

"Of course he was," Caroline protested. "You saw that throw."

"I also saw the catch. An amazing catch the receiver had to make with one hand because the quarterback overthrew him by a yard."

"It was one pass."

"There were a lot of passes like that, Mom."

Walking over, she sat on the arm of the chair and ran her fingers through his hair like she'd done when he was a kid. "How many tapes have you watched?"

"Enough." Enough to see the overthrown balls, the missed open receivers, an inability to read the defense. Not to mention his dad hadn't been able to throw across his body to the left. Or that he spent way too much time standing still in the pocket.

Weaknesses that hadn't stopped him from leading his high school team to the championship his senior year, but definitely would have been exploited in college, forget the pros.

"He was a good player," his mother insisted.

"Yeah, Mom. He was a good player at a small school. At a 4A school, he'd have been lucky to make the team and probably would never have left the bench." Frustrated, Zach picked up the remote from the trunk-style coffee table and clicked the video off before tossing it aside. His mother flicked on the floor lamp as he stood to face her. "All those years, talking

about how he would have had it made. College and a Heis-
man trophy and championship before moving on to the big
leagues." Sarcasm lifted his voice to a near shout by the time
he finished.

"Zach, please." Caroline tightened the belt on her already
cinched robe. "Why bring all this up now? I know he wasn't
the best father, but Dad's been dead for years. To be saying
these things now..."

Distress filled his mother's expression, and Zach exhaled,
forcing aside the lingering anger and gave her a hug. "I'm
sorry. I'm not trying to put him down or blame him for a past
no one can possibly change. I'm just trying to understand."
Running a hand through his hair, he sighed. "I was so sure I
had it all figured out."

His mother took his hand and led him back to the recliner.
"Had figured what out, sweetheart?"

Zach leaned back against the comfortable cushions, staring
at the now blank screen. An image reflected back at him—a
man seated in an armchair, trapped by the anger and bitterness he couldn't let go. "Dad was always talking about how
getting married and having a kid robbed him of his dream.
So I was sure that focusing on my dream, my goal was the
way to go. And for so many years, that's what I did. I didn't
let anyone or anything get in the way."

"Until Allison."

"Until Allison," he agreed with a small laugh, wondering
why he was even the least bit surprised that his mother had
figured that out before he had. "You know how I told you the
first time I saw her, she was cutting in front of my car?"

He'd been captured from the first glance through his wind-
shield and never managed to escape. "I'd never met anyone
like her. She was...different." He cringed at the inadequacy of
his words, but he'd never talked to his mother about a woman
before, so he hoped she'd cut him some slack. "I really thought

maybe I could have it all. But then when Knox gave the promotion to Bob Henderson, I knew that was impossible."

"But now the promotion's yours," Caroline reminded him, "and I assume Allison is no longer a distraction?"

Zach flinched at his mother's description even though he'd given her reason to think that way. Worse, he'd given *Allison* reason to think that way. And it occurred to Zach once more that if having the promotion was everything he'd ever wanted, he should have been a hell of a lot happier than he was.

Zach stood outside Bethany's townhouse, wondering what the hell he was doing. It was a question that had plagued him since he first got off the plane in San Francisco. He should have left a message at Allison's house and waited for her to call him back—*if* she called him back—instead of taking a chance and tracking her down at her sister's house. Her car was parked in the driveway, so he knew she was there, but he could still leave and no one would know he'd—

The door opened before he had a chance to turn back to his car, and then it was too late. Too late to run, too late to move. All he could do was stare at Allison. He soaked in the sight of her, the same way he had the desert sun after coming back from San Francisco fog. Her golden hair was pushed back with a thin headband, revealing her startled green eyes, her lips adorably parted in surprise. But her face was pale. She looked tired and—the bundle of what he'd dismissed as an armful of laundry gave a sudden squawk.

He looked closer and saw an almost impossibly small foot give an agitated kick. "Is that—"

A smile lit Allison's face, erasing any hint of exhaustion as she moved the blanket aside to reveal the infant's face. "I'd like you to meet Lilly Anne Armstrong."

Zach stared at the newborn in awe. The baby lifted eyelids

that looked to weigh a ton, blinked once, and fell back asleep. "She looks just like you," he whispered.

Allison shushed him. "Bethany's taking a nap, but you're lucky she didn't hear you say that."

"Well, of course, she looks like Bethany."

But as Allison led the way into the living room and bent to lay the infant in a bassinet tucked in the corner, it wasn't Bethany's baby he was picturing Allison holding. It was hers—theirs. The unexpected longing reached out and grabbed hold of his heart. A wife, kids, *family*... It was a life he never thought he wanted, but one he suddenly didn't know if he could live without.

Allison straightened to face him, but the thought of laying his heart on the line had him breaking into a cold sweat. Reaching for the first topic to come to mind, he said, "I didn't think your sister was due so soon."

"She wasn't. The baby came early."

"But she's okay?" It might have been a stupid question considering the hospital had already sent Bethany home, but what did he know about infants?

"She's perfect. And it's all thanks to you."

"Me? I don't think so. I really don't know your sister that well."

"Not like that," she said, shooting him that crooked smile that never failed to quicken his heart rate. But her expression sobered as she ran her hand over the baby's wispy blond hair. "Bethany had bought some pictures for the nursery and was trying to hang them when she lost her balance. She went into labor and couldn't get to the phone, but her purse was within reach. She activated the alarm from her key chain remote. If it hadn't been for that alarm... So, thank you."

He could still see the toll worry and fear had taken in the circles beneath her eyes. The baby gave a soft cry, and they both looked toward the bassinet. A tiny fist waved over the edge, but she settled back to sleep. "Has Bethany heard from her husband?"

"I called him from the hospital, and she's spoken to him a few times, but he doesn't want anything to do with Lilly."

Zach shook his head. "He'll regret that someday."

"I don't know…You can't force someone to want what you want."

"Allie—"

"I'm sorry about before, about the fight," she blurted out.

"So am I. So sorry." Relief poured over him, washing away the guilt he'd been carrying with him since their argument. He'd been such an idiot to blame Allison. The time they'd spent together had been the best of his life and worth more than any promotion. Had he really thought she'd stand in the way of his career? Allison had been a huge part of his success. With her at his side, Zach knew he could accomplish anything, but for the first time, business wasn't at the forefront. He had a different, far more personal goal—one he couldn't possibly achieve without Allison.

"And I'm sorry I didn't have the chance to tell you before you left, but I'm proud of you. You must be so excited about the promotion."

"About that—"

"Tell me everything. How was San Francisco? Did you meet the other board members? Will you get corner office with an amazing view? Oh, and what about a company car? Of course with all the traveling you'll be doing, a plane would be better, right? And I hope you have a razor-sharp assistant to keep you in line."

Zach frowned. Did Allison *want* him to take the promotion? To accept a job that meant constantly traveling, bouncing between three states? "What happened to me not being any good at managing?"

"I was wrong. Yes, you're a great salesman, but you'll be

a great sales manager, too. You love working at Knox Security, and it shows in everything you do."

Like the roller-coaster ride his emotions went on after first losing, then winning the promotion, Zach felt thrown for yet another loop. He didn't think the promotion was right for him; Allison did. He wanted to stay; Allison was telling him to go.

You can't force someone to want what you want.

Her words echoed in his mind, and suddenly Zach knew. Allison didn't *want* him to go, but she was afraid to ask him to stay, afraid to hold him back from everything she thought he wanted.

"I love you, Allie." At his words, her gaze flew to his, her green eyes wide. "I don't care about the promotion. I've told Knox I'll fill in until they find a replacement, but after that, I'm coming back here. To the job I love. To the woman I love."

"You can't!" Panic filled her eyes. "If you stay, you'll regret it. You'll resent me and—"

Zach caught her by the shoulders before she could make another pass by the couch. "I won't, Allie. I swear. I'm not Kevin, and I don't want to be like my father."

She exhaled a deep breath, but he could still feel the shudder of emotions bottled up inside her. "From what you've told me, you're the exact opposite of your father."

"I'd always thought that, but we're more alike than I want to admit. My dad spent his life blaming me and my mom for his professional failures. I was doing the same thing. Only in reverse. Using work as an excuse for the failures in my personal life. And then when I didn't get the promotion, I blamed you. I can't tell you how much I regret that. But I'll make it up to you. Believe me, I—"

"No."

"I'm going to—what?" His words stumbling to a halt, Zach realized Allison wasn't reacting the way he thought she would. He might not have much experience in spilling his heart or telling a woman he loved her, but he was pretty sure she was supposed to say "I love you" back. "Allison—"

"You've worked your whole career toward one promotion after another. Professional success is all you've ever wanted, and now you're telling me all that's changed?"

Zach swallowed, a numbing sense of shock taking over, holding off the pain he knew was coming. "It has changed. *I've* changed."

But Allison's disbelieving expression didn't, and she shook her head almost wildly. "After a few weeks? You're giving up a lifetime of goals after two weeks?"

Said out loud, the words did sound crazy, but in his heart, they rang true. A few weeks was long enough to change a lifetime if those days and nights were spent falling in love. Zach believed that with every beat of his heart, with every breath he took. But if Allison didn't, maybe it was because she didn't feel the same.

"Allie…"

The unspoken appeal caught in his throat, cut off by too many years of pleading for his father's time, attention, *love*.

How many times had he begged his old man to toss around the football despite his growing resentment for the game? And how many times had his father blown him off with a *not now* or *later* or stone-cold silence as he refused to even acknowledge his living, breathing son in favor of mourning a long-dead dream?

Eventually, Zach stopped asking, knowing he couldn't expect anything more than Nathan Wilder's painful slap of rejection. But he'd never, *never* expected it from Allison.

Allison sank onto the couch after Zach left. Every painful beat of her heart marked the time since he'd gone, a hollow sound that echoed inside her. She'd done the right thing, the *only* thing she could, and maybe someday, like when Zach was CEO of Knox, that thought would give her comfort. But for now the loss made the future, any future without Zach, seem lonely and empty.

He loved her. He loved her; he was willing to give up his goals and dreams *for her.* But how could she possibly let him do that when she knew what those dreams, what that promotion, meant to him? Zach had the chance to break free of his painful childhood, of his father's resentment and blame, to prove to himself he wasn't a failure.

How could she take that away from him? Allison swallowed. She couldn't. She loved *him* far too much.

"I take it Zach left," Bethany said from the doorway.

"I thought you were sleeping."

Bethany shrugged and walked over to the bassinet. A smile filled with a mother's love curved her lips as she lifted her daughter into her arms. One positive had come from Lilly's early appearance. With their mother still on vacation, Allison had been at her sister's side in the delivery room, and along the way, Bethany had let go of the bitterness and blame for all the times when Allison *wasn't* there to rejoice in a time when the two of them were as close as ever.

"It's a small place. Voices carry."

"Sorry we woke you."

Bethany shot her a wry sideways glance. "Not my point. I overheard you telling Zach to get lost."

"That is *not* what I did! I'm giving Zach what he wants. What he's always wanted."

"Sounded to me like he wants you."

"We've only known each other for a couple of months and until a few weeks ago, our relationship was strictly business. Zach has spent *years* working his way up."

Allison knew she couldn't expect her sister to understand. After all, Bethany hadn't heard all the times Zach vowed his career was the most important thing in his life, but Allison had. Again and again, he'd told her how he wouldn't let anyone or anything stand in his way. As much as she loved him, she couldn't bear the thought of that love being an obstacle, a hindrance, a burden....

"I can't let him throw that all away."

"So you're doing this for Zach?" Bethany asked.

Allison nodded. She loved Zach. She loved his determination, his drive, his focus. He could have followed in his father's footsteps, using his lot in life as an excuse to fail, but instead he'd risen above the challenges of his childhood. She'd been so wrong not to encourage him to go after the promotion from the beginning, and she refused to stand in his way now.

"Yes," she whispered. "I'm doing this for Zach."

After a brief moment of silence, Bethany baldly stated, "Yeah, I'm not buying it."

Stunned by her sister's cavalier attitude, Allison demanded, "What is that supposed to mean?"

Sitting on the couch beside Allison, Bethany smoothed a hand over her daughter's downy soft blond hair. "You know I didn't wake up one day and decide to—betray Gage the way I did." She held up a hand when Allison would have protested. "Don't, Allie. I know what I did, and there's nothing else to call it except a betrayal of his trust. But it wasn't an easy decision. I had to talk myself into it. And I did. By saying that I was doing what was best—for our marriage, for me, for Gage. I convinced myself I was right and Gage would come to see that, too. Only he hasn't, and I'm not sure he ever will."

"This isn't about what I want," Allison protested.

"I think it's about what you're afraid to want. You're afraid if you admit you love Zach and someday he chooses business over you, your heart will be broken again."

Losing Zach would be nothing like breaking up with

Kevin. Even though she'd thought she loved him, his betrayal had done more to hurt her pride than break her heart. But losing Zach...

"I am afraid," she admitted.

"Dad would be so disappointed in you."

The softly spoken words hit harder than any of Bethany's shouted accusations two weeks earlier. Allison hadn't cried when Zach left, afraid once she started she wouldn't stop, but tears burned her eyes. "How can you say that?"

"Because it's true. This isn't you, Allie! You were always the brave one, the adventurous one, remember? You always were willing to take a risk, to make that leap. But look at you now—the temp jobs, the meaningless hobbies..."

"I already told you that you were right about the job and the silly classes I've been taking." In trying to fix things with Bethany, Allison had denied the part of herself that thrived while working hard at a job she loved. She didn't want a career that consumed her life 24/7, but she needed a job that satisfied her and gave her a sense of accomplishment. "And I've given my notice at the temp agency."

"And that's a start. But what about now? What about Zach? Isn't it time you took another chance? Time to stop worrying about playing it safe and to just close your eyes and jump? It shouldn't even be that hard," her sister said with a smile. "Zach already went first."

"He did, didn't he?" Zach said he loved her. He wouldn't have given up on the promotion he'd worked so hard for unless he was sure. Sure of his feelings, sure of *them*. "Oh, Bethany! What have I done?"

"That's not nearly as important as what you do." Her sister waved a hand toward the door. "Go! Go after him."

Pausing only long enough to give Bethany and her newborn niece a hug, Allison jumped to her feet and grabbed her purse. Her heart was pounding as if she'd already raced a mile by the time she reached the front door. Afraid Zach was already long gone, she was scrambling for her phone and her keys as she stumbled down the steps from the townhouse. She caught the wrought iron banister before she lost her balance and looked up to see Zach's BMW parked across the street.

He stood with his hands braced on the gleaming black hood. His back was turned, but she could see stiffness in his shoulders and tension in his widespread stance. He looked like a man trying to shake off a body blow and she ached for what she'd put him through. But just when he looked beaten, Zach lifted his head and pushed off the car as if making some kind of decision—

She couldn't let him leave! She had to stop him. Allison sucked in a quick breath but instead of calling his name, she brought her fingers to her mouth and gave the sharp piercing whistle Zach once swore would stop traffic for miles. But she didn't care about traffic. All she wanted was to stop Zach.

He turned slowly, but instead of reaching for the door handle, he looked back toward the townhouse, back to Allison. Their eyes met for a brief second, and the next thing she knew, she was rushing into his arms. She didn't know which of them moved first, but it didn't matter. They'd made that leap together, and they'd landed right where they belonged.

Breathing in the scent of his skin, her hands fisted tight in his sun-warmed T-shirt and his arms wrapped around her waist, Allison didn't know how she'd thought even for a moment that she could live without Zach. She was a miserable failure when it came to playing things safe. Her heart simply hadn't been in the temp jobs she'd taken or the numerous hobbies she'd tried. But the risk of loving Zach, that was something she could throw herself into heart, body and soul, knowing he'd always be there to catch her.

"I love you, Zach." Pulling back to meet his gaze, she swallowed hard as the image of him with his hands braced in defeat against the car hood flashed through her thoughts. "I am so sorry I let you leave thinking I didn't."

"Hey, don't worry. I wasn't about to give up that easily. Like you said, I've worked for years to get what I want. Did you really think I'd quit on us after only a few weeks?"

The certainty in his blue eyes was the only answer Allison needed. Zach worked harder than anyone she'd ever known. He wasn't the kind of man to take the easy way out or to give up when times got tough.

"I should have realized you wouldn't. I just didn't be-lieve—couldn't believe—you'd give up your dreams for me."

"I'm not," he vowed. "You're everything I've ever wanted, and everything I was afraid to hope for. I love you. Do you really think any promotion could matter more than that?"

Overwhelming emotion bubbled up inside Allison, filling her with so much hope and wonder, she didn't know if she was going to laugh or cry or both. "You did a pretty good job at first convincing me that the promotion was all that mat-tered."

Zach shook his head ruefully. "I think I was trying to con-vince myself. Focusing on business, that was something I was comfortable doing. Something I knew I was good at. Maybe the only thing I was good at until I met you."

"No, Zach! There's much more to you than just work. Look at the way you've been mentoring Brett. We both know that isn't part of your job. And the way you took care of Sylvie," she added, remembering how quickly he'd responded to his former clients' call for help. "Even the way you wanted to carry on the charade of us dating in front of your mother. Maybe you were worried about the truth getting back to Riana Collins, but I think you knew seeing the two of us together would make your mom happy.... You're a great salesman, Zach, but you're an amazing man. And there's no reason why you can't be both."

Reaching up to cup his face in her hands, Allison said, "You should accept the promotion. I know it will mean a lot of travel, but we'll make it work. You've proved to me that you can do anything you put your mind to. You'll be the greatest VP Knox can imagine."

Zach gazed down at her as he turned his head and pressed a kiss into her palm. "And what if what I want to be the best husband you can imagine?"

He'd throw himself into the role. He'd devote every moment into being the best. Driven, dedicated and determined—that was the man Allison loved. Pure happiness broke free in a smile she didn't even try to contain. "Well, you better be sure because this isn't a temporary position."

"Oh, I'm fully prepared for a lifetime commitment."

"Then I'd have to say, Mr. Wilder, you're the only man for the job."

* * * * *

Harlequin®

COMING NEXT MONTH

Available October 25, 2011

#2149 CHRISTMAS IN COLD CREEK
RaeAnne Thayne
The Cowboys of Cold Creek

#2150 A BRAVO HOMECOMING
Christine Rimmer
Bravo Family Ties

#2151 A MAVERICK FOR CHRISTMAS
Leanne Banks
Montana Mavericks: The Texans Are Coming!

#2152 A COULTER'S CHRISTMAS PROPOSAL
Lois Faye Dyer
Big Sky Brothers

#2153 A BRIDE BEFORE DAWN
Sandra Steffen
Round-the-Clock Brides

#2154 MIRACLE UNDER THE MISTLETOE
Tracy Madison
The Foster Brothers

SPECIAL EDITION®

Harlequin® Special Edition® is thrilled to present a new installment in USA TODAY *bestselling author RaeAnne Thayne's reader-favorite miniseries,* THE COWBOYS OF COLD CREEK.

Join the excitement as we meet the Bowmans—four siblings who lost their parents but keep family ties alive in Pine Gulch. First up is Trace. Only two things get under this rugged lawman's skin: beautiful women and secrets. And in Rebecca Parsons, he finds both!

Read on for a sneak peek of CHRISTMAS IN COLD CREEK. *Available November 2011 from Harlequin® Special Edition®.*

On impulse, he unfolded himself from the bar stool. "Need a hand?"

"Thank you! I…" She lifted her gaze from the floor to his jeans and then raised her eyes. When she identified him her hazel eyes turned from grateful to unfriendly and cold, as if he'd somehow thrown the broken glasses at her head.

He also thought he saw a glimmer of panic in those interesting depths, which instantly stirred his curiosity like cream swirling through coffee.

"I've got it, Officer. Thank you." Her voice was several degrees colder than the whirl of sleet outside the windows.

Despite her protests, he knelt down beside her and began to pick up shards of broken glass. "No problem. Those trays can be slippery."

This close, he picked up the scent of her, something fresh and flowery that made him think of a mountain meadow on a July afternoon. She had a soft, lush mouth and for one brief, insane moment, he wanted to push aside that stray lock of hair slipping from her ponytail and taste her. Apparently he needed to spend a lot less time working and a great deal *more* time recreating with the opposite sex if he could have sudden random fantasies about a woman he wasn't even inclined to like, pretty or not.

"I'm Trace Bowman. You must be new in town."

She didn't answer immediately and he could almost see the wheels turning in her head. Why the hesitancy? And why that little hint of unease he could see clouding the edge of her gaze? His presence was obviously making her uncomfortable and Trace couldn't help wondering why.

"Yes. We've been here a few weeks."

"Well, I'm just up the road about four lots, in the white house with the cedar shake roof, if you or your daughter need anything." He smiled at her as he picked up the last shard of glass and set it on her tray.

Definitely a story there, he thought as she hurried away. He just might need to dig a little into her background to find out why someone with fine clothes and nice jewelry, and who so obviously didn't have experience as a waitress, would be here slinging hash at The Gulch. Was she running away from someone? A bad marriage?

So…Rebecca Parsons. Not Becky. An intriguing woman. It had been a long time since one of those had crossed his path here in Pine Gulch.

Trace won't rest until he finds out Rebecca's secret, but will he still have that same attraction to her once he does? Find out in CHRISTMAS IN COLD CREEK. Available November 2011 from Harlequin® Special Edition®.